"**H**UMBLE...but I call it home." The voice was deep, self-assured and slightly sardonic.

Vanessa whirled around. 'Twas the Viscount of Montlaine. Here was the portrait come to life. Here was the libertine, the suspected murderer. What could she say? Manners and breeding came to her rescue and restored her voice. "I...I'm sorry...truly. I know I have stumbled upon something you have been at pains to keep hidden...but when I saw what rumor has called a ghost...I could not credit it. You see, I don't believe in ghosts."

His satanic brow moved. "So you came sleuthing? With no concern for your safety?" His tone was contemptuous.

"Am I in danger, sir?"

He laughed. "You might very well be, if all they say about me is true."

Also by Claudette Williams:

AFTER THE STORM	23958	$1.75
BLADES OF PASSION	23481-9	$1.95
MYRIAH	23577-7	$1.50
SPRING GAMBIT	23891	$1.75
SUNDAY'S CHILD	23986	$1.75

Naughty Lady Ness

Claudette Williams

FAWCETT COVENTRY • NEW YORK

NAUGHTY LADY NESS

Published by Fawcett Coventry Books, a unit of CBS Pub-
lications, the Consumer Publishing Division of CBS Inc.

Copyright © 1980 by Claudette Williams

ISBN: 0-449-50045-4

Printed in the United States of America

First Fawcett Coventry printing: May 1980

10 9 8 7 6 5 4 3 2 1

Naughty Lady Ness

Chapter One

Brighton resounded tumultuously with its early-season patrons. All the haut ton who normally resided in London were beginning to flock to their fashionable homes, estates and respectable lodgings. The mood was festive in most parts of the Regent's favorite summer spot. However, one notable residence held a houseful of clucking servants, all of whom centered their misgivings and concerns around a maid they served—Lady Vanessa.

It was not without cause that they frowned and sighed mournfully, for this time their young mistress had plunged herself into a scrape that certainly would cause an erosion within their happy home. In fact, signs of that crumbling were already evident, for the lady's parents had that very morning (a week before they were expected) descended upon them in quiet rage.

The earl and countess of Grey had lost no time in packing up and leaving London to see to their wayward daughter. This was not without some irritation, for there was business the earl had not yet completed in

London. Clearly, though, this business had to be put aside if they were to see to their frivolous daughter and son.

In the brightness of a well-appointed library, behind tightly closed doors, sat the earl of Grey. His face was drawn in anger, and the smile that was one of his habitual characteristics was gone. His dark eyes were glinting, his tone was low and very stern. His countess stood off to one side. A handkerchief was wound between her fingers, and her lovely face was drawn in sadness. She did not like to see both her children so at odds with their father, but there was nothing for it—this time things had really gotten out of hand. She waited as her daughter moved to speak.

Glittering gray eyes looked imploringly across at the earl's rigidly outraged countenance, and an almost irresistible plea begged to shake his resolve. "Papa...try if you will...to understand...."

It did not serve. Perhaps she had chosen the wrong words, for indeed the earl felt that he had always bent over backward to understand his daughter's headstrong ways. He now felt, as did his wife, that they had been too lenient, and thus *scandal* was now facing them!

"How dare you, Vanessa! The problem is that I understand all too well!" He stood up as he replied and began pacing. He was losing control of his temper and wished to regain it. He sucked in breath and then rounded on his bright-eyed daughter. "It is beyond me, though, how you can have been so lost to your position, to your family's name.... Vanessa, how could you so embroil yourself in such an escapade without, it appears, even a second thought?"

"Papa...don't you see? My word! It is beyond every-

8

thing that you could be so much like those hypocrites out there!"

The countess took a step forward. "Vanessa... apologize to your father at once!"

Vanessa blushed. "Indeed, sir, I beg your pardon.... But only do think that since you came home, you have done nothing but scold, without hearing my part at all." She disliked being put in the position of child, and child she felt, pleading like this. It was most vexing, and her agitation showed as she worked her hands.

Her father studied her pixie face, found her sparkling eyes and quickly looked above to her auburn curls. He dared not allow himself to look into her face, for he wasn't about to let her charm him out of his wrath. "Don't you understand that it doesn't matter how you became the butt for gossip? What matters is that you did!"

"That is dreadful!" she returned at once. "If Ricky had done it, there would be backslapping and much jesting. It is not fair that because I am a female such a miserable fuss is being mucked up. Why... it is *archaic!*"

Lord Richard offered at this point, somewhat unwisely as it turned out, "I must say, Papa... Ness has a point, you know. After all, she couldn't let the challenge go unanswered, and she was most definitely challenged!"

The earl rounded on his son and stared with disbelief. His expression was such that the twenty-year-old lad was moved to blush and stammer quickly, "But... of course... I quite see now..."

"*You quite see now?* Heaven preserve my sanity!" the earl was moved to ejaculate. He turned to his count-

9

ess. "Will you tell me how *we* spawned such creatures?"

She smiled warmly. "I should think you best would know that answer, my love . . . if you think to your salad days."

He stopped and gave her a glimmer of a smile. Indeed, he remembered all too well his hot youth, and his daughter, even more than his son, gave every evidence of spending a similar youth. But he would not have it! Discipline—that was the ticket! He would discipline her. He and his wife had already worked out the details while in London. They had only to set them in motion. He returned his attention first to his son, for whom he still had quite a setdown.

"What I should like explained is how *you* could have allowed it, Richard! Why did you not take her place? I see that she felt her horse needed defending—I even, in my heart, sympathize with Vanessa on that point— but how could you have allowed her to race against Lord Walton herself?"

"Do not rake Ricky over the coals, Papa!" put in Vanessa at once. "He is my junior, after all, and could not stop me if he thought to, and he didn't think to because I am one and twenty and quite fully grown! Papa . . . the challenge was not only to my horse but to me, personally!"

This stalled her angry parent a moment, and he regarded her dubiously. "Really? Explain how so."

"You see . . ." She took a swallow of air. "We were at Aunt's rout last week, and overheard cousin Randy having something of an argument with Lord Walton. The next thing we knew, Walton was saying his bay gelding could outrun any steed Randy could think of. Well, Randy had only just seen me put Shadow to the test that morning and insinuated Shadow's name into the argument."

10

"Good boy, that Randy," put in Ricky with a shake of his fair hair. "Knows prime blood."

"Exactly . . . for you know what Walton is about his bay. Well, naturally Walton laughed and Randy got insulted. By that time, Rick and I were drawn into the argument. Walton said that there wasn't a man in Brighton could run Shadow against his bay and win. Well, Papa, I couldn't stand for that, could I? For you know what Shadow is. So I told him he was vastly mistaken."

"A prime setdown she gave him, Papa," put in Ricky, grinning, and then, seeing his father's glance, his smile vanished into a cough.

"I see," said her father, not a bit mollified by any of this.

"No, I don't think you really do. Papa . . . he said Shadow was naught but a lady's horse."

"Did he, by God?" returned her father in some surprise. "Why, Shadow has a reputation for anything else but a lady's nag!"

"Precisely . . . but he went rambling on saying that it was a rare jest if I thought I could beat his bay with my gentle mare. Papa . . . how could I stand for that?"

"No . . . I quite see you could not." Her father sighed. "Proceed. Then what did he say?"

"It was then that a large company assembled around us and began to titter. I couldn't let them, now could I? So, I told him that not only could a lady's mare beat his gelding, but that a lady could beat him!"

"Did you, by Jupiter? Upon my soul, Vanessa . . ." Her father was somewhat at odds with himself. His lass had spunk, and he was proud of her spirit. At the same time, she always managed to find one heady tumble after another. Something had to be done!

"I did not mean for it to happen, Papa . . . but I

11

couldn't allow Shadow to be slandered, and I couldn't allow myself to be lumped with all the misses of my day. *I won the race.* Does not that make it all very proper? I mean...Papa...*I won!*"

"And the only thing that saves you from total social ostracism is the fact that you are a daughter of the house of Grey and an heiress to boot!" returned her father uncompromisingly. He sighed again. "It isn't fair, is it? You are right—men can go about the countryside racing and behaving like lunatics, but the fact of the matter is, a lady *cannot*. You went outside the bounds of propriety when you raced on the open public road with Walton. Perhaps if you had kept to your own grounds...but you did not. *Wagers* were taken, my girl...your name was bandied about...don't you see?"

She sat back and thought about this. "Yes, Papa... I do...but..."

"I am afraid, my child, there are no buts, no excuses that may serve this time. This scrape can be handled only in one manner."

"How is that?" she asked on a note of concern, for there was something in his tone that worried her.

"Banishment, my love."

"What?" shrieked brother and sister at once. Vanessa glanced at her mother, who came to sit beside her and take up her daughter's hand.

"It won't be so very awful, my love," soothed the countess. "You, Vanessa, will be sent off to friends of ours in Cornwall. It was arranged with Lady Penrod when we were in London and first heard the rumors of your...trouble here in Brighton."

"But...but Mama..."

"You like Lady Penrod—at least you have always said so—and she will be most pleased to have your company this summer," returned the countess gently.

"Too bad, Ness," offered her brother sympathetically.

"*You*, Rick, will accompany her," put in his father.

"What?" It was a shriek indicating great pain. "But Papa ... only think ... *Cornwall!*"

"Cornwall," returned the earl rigidly. "Absence is a great balm. The gossip mongers will have to find another piece of meat to chew ... and make certain, they will. You will not return until it is time for you, Rick, to attend Cambridge and Ness to enter the London season."

"Oh, Papa ... surely Rick does not have to go. It isn't fair. What good does it do to send Rick?"

"You cannot make the journey alone, girl ... and it will be nice for you to have him with you in the country. Besides, it will keep him out of trouble, for there is bound to be some talk about you, Ness, and knowing Rick as we do, he would no doubt end in using his fives to defend your honor. No, it is decided. You will leave for Cornwall, Wadbridge on the Water, by the end of the week."

"And in the meantime, my love, you will confine your movements to the house," put in the countess.

"Oh, my God! Do you mean I cannot ride Shadow? I cannot go for walks?"

"Not without your brother in attendance and only in the off hours ... away from town."

"Very well, then, but only let Rick return to Brighton after he deposits me in Cornwall."

"I wouldn't do anything so shabby as to return without you!" put in her brother staunchly.

"Are you suggesting that I am sending your sister off somewhere undesirable, Richard? It is no such thing. Really, I am no monster."

"Of course you are not, Papa ... and I am very sorry

13

I have once again given you and Mama cause to fret. I shall endeavor to be more the paragon of virtue in the future." She got to her feet. "Now... if you have nothing more, I should like to retire to my room."

Her parents could see she was in a temper. They didn't believe for a moment that she meant to be anything but herself, and in unison they sighed. "You may go, child," said her father, wishing in that moment that one of her many suitors had managed to win her heart. What the girl needed was marriage and a family of her own!

On the eve of Vanessa Grey's fateful race, odd doings were afoot in Cornwall. The night was well lit with a full moon and bright stars and yet strangely foreboding as though in expectancy of what was to come. And at Montlaine Castle a small world was crumbling.

"Step lively, m'lord... mistress... fer them coming up the hill be fearful angry and out fer blood," cried Epps, the viscount's man.

The viscount of Montlaine bent his head against the wind and held the gentle girl beside him closer still as he pulled her along the stark drive that led to their stables. They said not a word until they had reached their horses and begun tacking up. Then the girl spoke, pushing aside her hood to exhibit a crop of dark waves and the face of a young maid.

"But Bret... Bret... you cannot mean to run! You must stand against their charges and prove them false!" She was much agitated.

He took hold of her chin, and she was struck by his wild good looks. His raven hair fell in waves about his head. His dark eyes were nearly as black as the brows that jutted to a peak, giving him that satanic countenance. If she hadn't known better, at this moment she

14

could have mistaken him for the devil they accused him of being. "No, Mary child. I'll not allow the name of Montlaine to face a mob. There is never any reasoning with a rabble out for revenge."

"But what will you do?"

"There is no time now to explain. You take this note along with you and make for Lady Penrod's, where you will be safe enough. They'll not come for you there."

"Can you be sure? Oh, Bret...they are saying you are the devil and I one of your minion witches....Bret...I am so frightened."

He hoisted her into her saddle. "Keep a tight rein...keep her head up and don't take a reckless pace. That's the lass." With which he sent her into the night.

His groom moved with impatience. "M'lord...up wit' ye. There's no time...no time..."

The black stallion snorted as the viscount of Montlaine took the reins and jumped nimbly into his saddle. He eased him onto the drive, but it was already too late, for the mob had arrived and began swarming, making his exit very near impossible.

Mobs seldom have leaders, but this one did. The magistrate of Wadbridge, astride a chestnut, sat straight in his seat and called out, "Halt! My Lord...I must ask you to go no farther."

Silence. It was as though the wind itself calmed in anticipation of the viscount's response. He laughed. "Gentlemen, you are on my land, trespassing...and you dare to order *me* about!"

The magistrate squirmed uncomfortably. He held up the warrant, yet even so, he felt himself on shaky ground. "I have here a warrant, sir...my lord...for your arrest!"

"Do you? And what is the charge?"

"Murder, ye divil ye!" cried a distraught woman,

15

stepping out of the crowd. This set up a sizable murmur at her back. "Ye killed me daughter . . . ye seduced the poor child to yer devilry . . . made her one of yer witches . . . and then cast her aside. She died in a convulsion . . . from one of yer spells, she did. . . ."

"Did she, by God? Whom are we speaking of, may I ask? And why the deuce am *I* being charged with her death?"

"She was Miss Melony Fry. You know her, my lord, for I myself have seen you dallying with the poor girl in the fields. 'Twas yer own unmistakable pendant that she held in her hand."

"My pendant? I lost that more than three . . . four days ago. If you had come up to the house first, you could have questioned my aunt, my servants. They would have attested to that fact. Do you realize what you have done? Do you? Coming up here with that rabble at your back? By Jupiter, sir, I shall have your head and that of the idiot who issued the paper you wave at me now!" He spoke with enough authority and self-assurance to make the magistrate quiver.

However, this was no time to back off and look the dunce. The crowd called for action, and he was not about to hold them off at cost of his own neck. They had heard that a warrant for his lordship's arrest had been issued. Somehow, they had heard and they had collected and followed him to this point. It had been rather exciting, but he could see now, it had been a grave mistake to allow it. This would not look well with his superiors.

"What you say is all very well, my lord . . . but, I must still ask you to come with me, quietly."

"Come wit' ye? What . . . so as they can be dazzled wit' his name? No, Rawkens . . . we be of a mind to 'ave

16

him now!" shouted a man, waving his pitchfork high in the air.

"Aye," growled another man, pushing forward in the crowd. He twirled a noose up high. "Bring 'im off that divil 'orse of 'is and 'ang 'im 'igh!" He turned to his fellows and commanded them with gestures to pick up the chant.

There is something about a mob. One loses one's identity and feels a part of a greater whole and consequently more powerful. Violent feelings inspired action, and another picked up a stone. It was flung high and skimmed by the viscount's hatless head. A second stone followed, this time catching the rump of the black stallion. Unused to such treatment, the proud steed rose on its hindquarters and pawed the air. Its whinny shook the air, and for a moment the mob was spellbound by the sight.

Midnight's master took the reins and urged his horse into action. This was no time to stand his ground and attempt reason. In a split second rider and horse were charging through the rabble, making a path and diving into the night.

The magistrate had been frightened by the growing tension that surrounded him. He had retreated in the face of violence. However, he could not allow the viscount to escape. He was to come in for questioning, and he would not have the law flouted. He had with him two mounted officers, and with his hand up he ordered them to follow the viscount. In addition, some of the villagers had come on horseback, and they too joined in the chase. Shouts, shaking fists and flying hooves, driven by a frenzy only blind irrationality can produce.

The viscount glanced back and shook his head. Worse, so much worse than he had anticipated. The solution? He saw only one, and that an extremely unpleasant one. He urged his stallion onward, the pace a heady dangerous gallop over the moors. The case against him would be strong, and he would need help, help and time, if he was ever to clear his name. Both were things he lacked at the moment. He veered southeast, heading for Bodmin Heights.

The magistrate could just see him... but what the deuce? The viscount was heading for Bodmin Heights! There was no escape there, only the cliffs... and below them the ocean with its jutting boulders. Why would he race his horse in that direction? Had he gone mad?

Shouts were carried by the night wind, their fury dispersed on the moors as the viscount jumped off his steed. One moment, he had but one moment to stroke his stallion's nose and speak soothingly into the alert ears. They had seen much together, he and this horse. He had trained the animal for many things things....

"Home, Midnight! Home!" With which he slapped the horse's rump hard.

Midnight understood the command and he knew his way, yet he hesitated and pawed the earth. "No, Midnight... *home!*" Again he slapped the horse, harder still, and this time Midnight shot out. The viscount stood a moment more watching the retreating dark form, and then he was facing the onrushing mob.

It had been a long time since he had last dived into the treacherous waters below. The current was deadly and the rocks far worse, and this time he would have to appear as though he were falling. There was every chance he would not survive! He grinned wide and stepped back as the mob closed in.

"Get 'im, lads!" screamed one panting officer, irritated with having to take on a dangerous chase over the moors at night. His supper and wife awaited him, and he would have the thing over with.

"I think not!" said the devil, stepping farther back and then suddenly releasing a scream as real as the event—for he was reeling backward into space and over the edge of Bodmin Heights!

The hunters ran toward the edge of the cliff. They felt cheated, strangely elated, and afraid all at once. For all their earlier bravado, the viscount had been a Montlaine, and there was no telling what would come of this night's work. They stood, the mob, robbed of their prize, and stared into the blackness. Below, only the ocean's waves beat against rocks and granite cliffs.

"You saw!" demanded the magistrate. "It was an accident! He slipped . . . his death was an accident . . ."

"Upon my soul!" agreed his officer. "That it was, sir!"

"And good riddance!" answered Farmer Fry, finding his voice. "He took m'girl's life as surely as though he put the knife to her heart, he did. The divil be dead, fer it's well known not he nor any of his familiars can survive the brine."

"Aye . . . and if he be man, he can't survive the current, nor the rocks neither," added the officer.

And still they stood staring a goodly while, just to be sure!

Chapter Two

An unpleasant week passed for Lady Vanessa Grey as her parents made arrangements to pack her off to their friend Augusta, Lady Penrod. For the most part Vanessa found herself confined to the house and its limited grounds. She was unable to attend the assemblies and routs that she had always found even after three London seasons vastly entertaining.

She pouted a great deal of the time and she put up many a logical argument, but nothing would move her father from his decision. Even the morning visitors that flocked to see her when she did not appear at the assemblies were turned away with the tidings that Lady Vanessa was suffering a bout of fatigue. So it was that she actually came to look forward to the journey to Cornwall.

At first, this proved to be something of a treat. She was allowed her steed, Shadow, and she used her for most of the day, riding beside her brother and cousin on the open pike. They passed through Romney Marsh, and she told her male relatives exciting stories of the smugglers that used to dwell in the region and cause havoc among the farmers. It was common knowledge that smuggling still persisted and now found favor among the locals.

Anxiously, almost wistfully, they awaited a chance meeting with the flaskers of Romney, but not a sign of them did they see. No, and not a highwayman gave them the opportunity of defending their belongings or their lives. Dull sport indeed. They had been seven days on the road, and though Cornwall earth was now being taken they felt deflated and somehow unjustly cheated. The week's journey had done nothing to stimulate their spirits, for they had not met with adventure and the weariness of daily travel had descended heavily upon them.

Randall, son of the house of Southvale and cousin to Richard and Vanessa of Grey, remarked upon the rugged harshness of the geography with some distaste, "Damn, but didn't I tell you it would be outlandish?"

"Yes, but only think, Randy ... at low tide we shall be able to take our horses across to St. Michael's Mount from Marazion. Buck up, for I am certain we shall find endless things to do," offered Vanessa happily.

"Yes ... well ... I seem to remember your saying how exciting this trip would be, and it wasn't!" he returned sulkily.

"But Randy, how poor-spirited of you. Didn't we pass through Romney Marsh ... and didn't we see the wild ponies of the New Forest and then again in Devon ... and such scenery we have gazed on! Enough to take your breath away!" she retorted.

"Scenery! Bah! Just look around you . . . rocks, more rocks . . . and sea . . ."

"Stubble it, Randy!" admonished Ricky impatiently. "I explained to you at the outset, and I think it high time you adapted to this venture!"

Blue eyes glared into blue eyes. These two male cousins were much alike in appearance. Both fair, both in the style of Corinthians, and friends since infancy. Jesting and jousting alternately was a perpetual pastime.

"You hoodwinked me, is what!" snapped Randy. "How I came to be a part of this . . ." He motioned in the air.

"You are a part of it because the whole thing was your fault from the start!" retorted Ricky. "It was you who brought Shadow's name into the argument."

"There you go, putting the blame at my door."

Vanessa sighed. She glanced behind to see that the carriage, carrying a quantity of luggage, a driver, postilion and her elderly maid, was moving along steadily. She was tired of the boys' bickering, for they had been going at it for the last two days over various subjects. "I'm going to ride up ahead. I shan't be long." With which she urged her horse off into a canter.

Neither lad looked her way. Ricky was busy controlling his temper. "Damn! It's so simple, Randy . . . why can't you see? If you hadn't mentioned Shadow, hadn't said Shadow could beat Waltons blasted blood . . . actually, the entire thing was your fault!"

"What? Should I let Walton spout off without answering him?"

"Doesn't change a thing. Look how it turned out!"

Randy nearly spluttered. There was no winning this argument. The fact was that Ricky had him nearly convinced that it was indeed his fault that they were now in Cornwall. It wasn't how he had planned to spend his summer, but then, once he had heard Ricky was off for the devilish place, he knew he too would be.

Vanessa rode on until she came to a cluster of pines and what appeared to be a private path. Up farther she could see the brick-and-iron gate with the name of Penrod emblazoned upon it. Therefore, the path led onto Penrod land ... how intriguing! She turned her horse and took it at a sedate jog when something caused her horse to start. Shadow was ever alert, and quickly Vanessa scanned the wood.

A face with large dark eyes. The eyes showed fear and then suddenly vanished. "My word ..." breathed Vanessa, amazed. "Hallo!"

There was no answer. The face was gone. A chill tingled Ness's spine, and she pivoted her horse round. She sucked in teeth and took off at a heady pace, making for the open road. There was something frightening about this wood ... about that face and those large sad eyes.

Randy looked about him. No sign of Vanessa. She had been gone quite a spell. "Where the deuce is she, Rick? Been gone awhile, you know. Don't like it ... won't have it! Don't want Uncle coming down on us in Cornwall and carting us off God knows where!"

"Lord, Randy ... didn't even see her go. Look, she can't have gone far."

"No? It's her side trips I'm worried about. Cost us half a day when she decided to explore Romney Marsh."

"Yes, but it ended at the Mermaid Inn, and that was well worth it! Spank-up good time we had there."

Randy reflected on this. "Ay, but still, Rick ... perhaps you had better ride up and see what she is about—"

"Hold!" Rick indicated with his chin that a rider was coming around the bend. "Lord ... girl, slow down!" he called.

She drew up to an inch and was breathing hard. "Rick ... oh, Rick, the oddest thing just occurred. It quite gave me the jitters!"

"Where the deuce have you been?" demanded Randy.

She gave him an arched look, and had he or Rick been other than brother or cousin they might have been smitten, as had many of their gender. However, their relationships saved them this fall and enabled them to exhibit stern faces.

"Oh, now don't look so out of reason cross!" she teased. "Only do listen ... I found Penrod Tower, 'tis but up the road a bit. However, just before the gate, there is a narrow wooded path. I took it ... just to explore, you see ... when suddenly from behind a thicket of bushes peeped this face ... a girl, oh, no more than fifteen or so, and her eyes ... huge round dark eyes, and she appeared frightened."

"Probably was with you charging down on her with that mad mare of yours!" bantered her brother.

"No, no, Rick. I'm serious. The girl looked sad and scared all at once and then ... poof, she vanished!"

"I don't like this! Don't like vanishing girls ... especially in this part of the country. Cornwall is full of witches, you know," put in Randy knowingly.

"Stop it, silly. Witches indeed! There are no such things," admonished Vanessa.

"Used to be," returned Randy, not to be put aside.

"No ... what there used to be were witch hunts and witch trials. There hasn't been a witch trial in years and years ... not, I think, since Grandfather was born," said Vanessa.

"Maybe not a legal one, Ness ... but I think out here

and up north there are still an awful lot of people that are afraid of witches," said her brother.

"Hmmm. Well, the coach is catching up to us. Perhaps I had not better arrive on horseback. I'll tether Shadow and climb in with Millie. Propriety, you know." She laughed and put up her hand for her coach to halt.

Rick glanced at Randy. "What's the matter?"

"Don't know ... just know I don't like this place ... don't like vanishing girls ... and ..."

"Randy?"

"Yes?"

"Do shut up!"

Lady Penrod was a woman of many impeccable qualities. Quick wit, warm-heartedness and understanding were among these. Ah, to a girl of fifteen who was flushed, frightened and in a tither, these assets were gold.

"But Lady Penrod ... she saw me ... I don't know how I came to be so *stupid!* All I could do was stand frozen and stare at her."

"Hush, child ... you must calm yourself," soothed her ladyship, putting her strong arm around the girl's shoulder and pulling her toward the settee. "Now, who saw you?"

"I don't know ... she was quite beautiful ... riding this snowy gray mare ... right up our wooded path. Oh my lady, what shall I do?"

Lady Penrod sighed. It was bound to happen, of course. Mary of Montlaine had come to the tower in her absence. Luckily, the Penrod butler who cared for the Cornwall estate year-round was related to the Montlaine butler, and both were faithful. The staff under the Penrod man was loyal to him, and so they had closeted Mary of Montlaine with none in the village the wiser. Mary had been at Penrod Towers a week in hiding, and then her ladyship arrived and they had decided between them to keep her on in secret. She patted her charge's hand.

"Perhaps, dear, it is time to send you off to my sister's care in London." Inwardly she longed for her husband. He would have known exactly what to do, but he was gone now three years. She would just have to manage this herself!

"Oh, no! You cannot!" cried the girl, much distressed.

Lady Penrod eyed her. "I think your brother would have agreed with me, child."

A large tear formed in the girl's dark eye. "I still can't believe he is really ... dead."

"Is that what you were doing out? Mary ... you must not be seen! You just simply cannot keep going to Bodmin Heights! What do you expect to find there?"

"I ... I don't know ... I look out to the sea ... oh, ma'am ... he couldn't have survived the fall ... the waters there are treacherous and the jutting rocks ... oh, ma'am ... but then where is his body?"

"Child, child ... it is well known that the tide could have taken him. . . . Don't dwell on it. You must forget."

"Forget? How can I forget what the villagers have done to us? Bret survived the war ... all those years in Spain ... only to come home and be accused of witchcraft and murder! How can such things be?"

"I don't have an answer for you, love. I don't know what has been happening here this past year. But somehow we shall try and clear his name. If I only knew where ... how to begin ..."

The sitting-room door opened wide and Toby, the

Penrod butler, stepped within. "I am so sorry to bother you, m'lady . . . but we have a bit of a problem."

"Oh? What is it, Toby?"

"Guests, m'lady . . ."

"Guests . . . who, pray?" She was genuinely surprised, as she did not expect anyone at this hour of the day.

"Lady Vanessa Grey, the Lord Richard of Grey and their cousin, Randall of Southvale. I took them to the library and had refreshments sent to them there."

Lady Penrod put a hand to her temple and pressed ever so lightly. "My God! I had quite forgotten." She turned to her young charge and took up her hands. "Now listen to me carefully, child, for we have something of a muddle ahead of us. When I was in London, Lady Grey's family were in a bit of a scrape. They were about to send off their daughter, who had displeased them, to relatives in the north. I felt I could do more with Ness here . . . never mind the details now . . . I had no way of knowing then what was towards here at Penrod, or that you would be here waiting for me and in need of sanctuary." She shook her head. "This is going to be difficult . . . for Ness has such an inquiring eye . . . little escapes that minx . . . and I daren't inform her of your troubles, for she would think it only right that she charge headlong into battle on your behalf. Her parents sent her to me to stay out of trouble, not find more of it. Oh dear . . ."

"I am so sorry, ma'am . . . will you send me away?" the voice was scarcely audible.

She gave the girl a warm hug. "Send you away indeed! No, of course not. . . . But don't go down the hall to your quarters . . . take the cupboard passage . . . and do stay out of sight. We shall find a solution."

"Yes, ma'am..."

Her ladyship waited, watching Mary press a knob that controlled a spring in the wainscoting. The half-sized door opened and Mary bent to take the hidden corridor to her wing. Her ladyship heaved a sigh and turned to Toby. "Well, Toby old friend...let us not keep our guests waiting."

Chapter Three

"Ho there... Willard!" a thunderous voice touched with raillery called the grizzled elderly gentleman within the small confines of the gatekeeper's cottage. "Ho there, ye old dog, open up for Montlaine!"

Willard set down his pot of hot water with a sigh. There was no end to it this day! Lord, if it wasn't one thing, it was another, what with her ladyship saying he had to help with the gardening... and then his having to rush back to open the gates for them flash young gentry! And now just when he was about to relax with a hot toddy...

He stuck his head out the door and saw the large black coach with gold leafing and a coat of arms depicting the house of Montlaine.

"Huh!" he grumbled to himself. "That ain't no Montlaine... maybe quality blood... but never a Montlaine..."

"Well, be ye coming, whiskers?" laughed the driver atop the coach.

Willard allowed the driver a grimace. "Hold yer

31

'orses, ye resty ole man! Can't ye see I'm coming?'"

The gate was swung wide and he stood aside to watch as the Montlaine driver urged his pair of bays forward. He slowed as he passed the gatekeeper and winked. "I'll be down in a brace o' snaps and we'll 'ave a cup, eh?"

Willard relented. "Aye ... but what news of Montlaine?" He was a Penrod man, had been for most of his fifty-odd years. Penrod and Montlaine went back in time for longer than he remembered, and he was staunchly loyal to tradition.

"No news, old friend. Looks like his lordship has gone to his maker this time ... looks like ..." mused the driver sadly.

"Bad times these," noted Willard with a shake of his head.

"Driver!" a woman's voice called shrilly, rapping at the ceiling of the coach with a cane for emphasis. "What are you waiting for? Move on! Move on!"

"Ay, Mrs. Echworth ..." And with a sigh the Montlaine coach ingressed on Penrod Land.

Within the carriage, three individuals contemplated the errand they had offered themselves to. The thoughts of each were much at variance with those of the others.

"I don't see the purpose of this visit, Mama!" Pretty lips pouted, making the attractive face less so. Sheila Echworth brought up a gloved hand and patted her light ginger-colored curls, adjusted her straw bonnet and stared out on Penrod Park with something of envy in her pale hazel eyes.

Mrs. Echworth regarded her daughter from narrowed eyes. Sheila was nearing her twenty-first year and she had failed to snare a worthwhile prize. It was a disappointment, but then the girl had not had the advantage of a fortune to launch her . . . until now. "Sheila . . . may I remind you that we are very much concerned about our cousin Mary. She has been missing since that terrible night . . . and I have reason to believe that Lady Penrod may know where she is."

"Why should we care where she is?" It was all so boring. She gazed out on lovely green lawns, magical flower beds, an elegant gazebo, and then the Tower itself, with its pretty turrets and fairytale fashion. It was too bad Montlaine was so different.

The gentleman beside her affected a sneer. Brummel himself would have applauded its style. His dress too was not to be despised, as he was clothed in a simple coat of dark-blue superfine and gray breeches. His face was pleasant, his waves à la Brutus were a maze of variegated shades of yellow and his eyes serenely gray.

"There is every reason on earth we should wish her with her brother, my dear, but alas, I fear Mother is correct. She is probably safely tucked within the walls of Penrod."

"Stop it, Orson! We have no reason to wish Mary ill," admonished his mother severely. She smoothed the silk of her dark-gray mourning gown and avoided her son's eye.

"Oh . . . don't we? May I remind you that it is my *older* brother who shall inherit Montlaine . . . that he shares his inheritance with our dear cousin Mary?"

"Oh yes, but she is only a child, after all . . . and besides . . . " Mrs. Echworth cut herself off, for they had arrived before the great doors of Penrod Tower. Already the Penrod footmen were hurrying forward to open the door of the coach.

"And besides . . . Mary is missing," put in her son on a whisper.

Mother and son exchanged a strong look, full with

a meaning they thought lost on Sheila. She took note of it with a twinge of irritation, and because she wanted them to realize she was up to their intrigues, she put in archly, ". . . or will be?" and smiled to see them turn around to look at her sharply.

There was no time for further comment as they were ushered politely into the house to await an audience with Lady Penrod.

Lady Vanessa had been doing a tour of the room, talking all the while, expounding her views on the hypocrisy of society and ending on a heavy sigh, ". . . and to think that instead of rewarding me for a job well done—for I beat that canting park saunterer—I am banished to Cornwall!" She turned on her hostess, a woman she had long ago learned to confide in. "Where is the justice in that, Guss?"

Augusta Penrod personally saw nothing shocking in a female taking on a race and winning it, especially a female whose name and position in society were unassailable. However, the laws of the ton forbade such hoydenish escapades. She reached out and took up Ness's hand. "My love, your lease of infancy was up some years ago. You know as well as I that justice does not always prevail!"

Vanessa sighed and turned on her brother. "And you! You are a man . . . you don't think I did something wicked, do you?"

He was quick to assure her that he did not and called on their cousin to add his voice to this proclamation, for his sister gave every indication of taking on a cause . . . and in the wilds of Cornwall that could only mean one thing—trouble!

Pleased with their response, Vanessa was next about to suggest that they begin to actively do something about such inequalities when her eye lit upon an embroidery only half started. She had done something much the same many years ago...and for no better reason she was reminded of the frightened young girl's face in the woods. "Guss...by the by...I saw..."

Once again Toby entered the room and announced the Echworths of Montlaine. However, the butler's face went rigid with disapproval when Mr. Orson, closely followed by mother and sister, swept imperiously past and intruded without awaiting his escort.

If Orson Echworth's tactic was meant to catch her ladyship by surprise and thus find his cousin Mary, it was for naught. If he was disappointed, he hid it well, and if his reprehensible entrance offended the proprieties, he made up for it with his poise and mannerly bow over Lady Penrod's outstretched hand.

"In or out of London, my lady, you are ever the irresistible magnet." His voice was low, flirtatious.

Augusta Penrod had never been a beautiful woman. She had never needed to be, for she had the wisdom to use what nature had given her. She clothed her tall frame with elegance and style, she allowed her wit to entertain and her charm to warm even the coldest of hearts. She was quite used to even younger men paying her court, and Echworth and his brother were ever prominent on the London scene. She liked him well enough. "Scamp!" She rapped his hand and turned to his mother and sister. These two she actively disliked; however, she was always the perfect hostess.

"Mrs. Echworth...Sheila...how good to see you are out and about." She turned to Toby and requested him to bring a fresh batch of hot tea, before turning to Vanessa. She smiled to herself as she saw that Orson Echworth had already discovered the beautiful Vanessa. Lord Richard of Grey and Randall of Southvale had jumped to their feet the moment Mrs. Echworth and her daughter had entered the room. Impatiently they waited for the introduction before hurriedly attempting to seat themselves beside the pretty new arrival.

The amenities passed quickly before an uncomfortable momentary silence ensued. Mrs. Echworth was at a loss. She was not sure just how to broach the question of Mary. She hedged a moment, all too aware that Lady Vanessa was studying her from beneath dark lashes. However, it had to be done.

"Lady Penrod ... I hesitate to speak of our troubles before your guests..."

Ness's finely arched brow rose. A mystery? Scandal in Cornwall? It was of course too funny. She felt a giggle tickle her, restrained herself and managed in a controlled tone, "Would you like us to leave? I am sure we have much to do before dinner..."

Lady Penrod's emotions ruled. She disliked Mrs. Echworth. Instant umbrage in her heart objected to dismissing Vanessa and the boys. Mrs. Echworth's troubles were common knowledge. Ness would hear about it sooner or later, it might as well be now!

"Don't be silly, love. Mrs. Echworth has no objection to your remaining to finish your tea." She smiled sweetly at the pudgy face of Mrs. Echworth and waited.

"It is Mary!" blurted out the woman. "We don't know where she is ... there are papers to sign ... legal ..."

"And of course we are worried about our cousin," put in Orson gently. "She is, after all, only a child. Where can she have gone?"

"I would think perhaps to relatives in London. I heard talk among the servants..." offered her ladyship, wondering why it was she was not blushing, chilling because she was not sure why she lied.

"But ..." said Orson, quietly, so very quietly, with

36

a hint of puzzlement, "*we* are Mary's closest relatives."

"But you were at Montlaine," returned her ladyship simply, "and Montlaine no longer was safe for Mary . . . as I understand." She sighed. "It is really too bad that I was still in London at the time. If I had been at Penrod, she would have come to me."

"And of course, she would not have come here . . . in your absence?" A faint suggestion that he was not sure of this.

She smiled at him. "If she could not feel safe at Montlaine, among her closest relatives, among her own servants . . . how then could she feel safe at Penrod without my authority in attendance? No, make no mistake . . . she has gone to London."

Mr. Echworth stood, and his mother followed suit. They were not convinced but they could not take it any further. Again he bent over her ladyship's hand.

"I am sorry we have had to trouble you when you were entertaining."

"No trouble, Orson . . . I was meaning to come by and see you. Tell me, is it true that Midnight broke out of his stall and cannot be found?"

"Yes, I am afraid so . . . at least, according to Epps. Personally, I think he sold the horse for a pretty sum and pocketed the money!" sniffed Mrs. Echworth.

Toby appeared with the tea tray. "Oh, do stay and have tea with us," urged Lady Penrod politely.

"No, I think not. I should like to get home and jot off a letter to Duncan. He is in London, you know . . . perhaps he can find Mary," returned Mrs. Echworth. She turned to discover her daughter getting on nicely with what she would have termed the biggest marriage prizes on the market. Sweetly she smiled. "Come along, Sheila . . ."

Mr. Echworth surveyed Lady Vanessa Grey. She had

remained quietly in the background, very much as though she were bored with conversation that held no interest for her. And then he discovered her eyes. Glittering diamonds with depths he would have liked to explore. He moved her way and found her smile engendered a very real one across his own face. A beauty was this auburn-haired chit!

"I hope, Lady Vanessa . . . we shall have the pleasure of your company at Montlaine." His voice was low.

She glanced at her brother and cousin fawning over Sheila Echworth and let go a light chuckle. "The male members of my family are sure to be there sooner than you expect, sir."

His glance followed hers, and he grinned. She had a sense of humor. He inched toward her brother, drawing her along as he moved. "Lord Richard . . . I was attempting to persuade your sister to visit with us at Montlaine. See what you and your cousin can do to bring her to us tomorrow."

Under her breath she allowed her musical voice to tickle him: "Very neat, Mr. Echworth!"

He turned to face her full. "Wasn't it, though?" He bent over her hand. "My lady . . ."

A few moments later, much to Sheila's distress and regrets, the Echworths had gone, and Lady Vanessa's hands went to the blue silk that covered her hips as she rounded on her hostess.

"Well, Guss! What was all that about?" A finger went up with the warning, "And you needn't try to do me up brown, for I shall find out in the end, you know!"

Chapter Four

Epps waited for the Montlaine coach to round the bend of the long, winding barren drive that led away from Montlaine Castle. Beneath his breath he cursed the Echworth family, for in his estimation, the lot of them were absolutely worthless. In the crook of his arm a bundle rested as he scurried over the rough-hewn land toward the moors and Bodmin Heights.

There were none that knew the moors as he did, and he had shown all their secrets to Bret of Montlaine when the lad was still in shortcoats. He had to hurry now, though, before someone saw him. Before them Echworths returned from Penrod. Lord sanctify his mission, thought the wiry man as he scrambled over yellow wildflowers and the evergreen thrusts of heather nearing its blooming power. Swiftly he put scarcely traveled terrain behind him. No one came to these moors. They were superstitious in Cornwall, and this particular stretch of moor was associated with lewd tales of witchcraft. More so now, since the night Montlaine had lost his life. Rumor had it that Montlaine's soul had found the demon horse Midnight and that together they rode the moors of Bodmin seeking revenge! He smiled to himself over the thought.

Down over the ragged rocks, down toward the narrow beach, around the boulders... toward the worst of the jutting rocks, there crouched a broad-shouldered man whose black cape whipped backward in the force of the sea wind. A welcome sight, the viscount of Montlaine!

The viscount was bent in upon his knee, an elbow rested there. His other arm relaxed at his side. His black eyes seemed mesmerized by the crashing waves before him. His satanic brows were drawn in contemplation of his fate, of the events that had brought him to this distinction in time. Much of it was due to his own wayward carelessness, his own hardness of heart, his own selfish whims and his own blindness to those closest to him.

A sound, the pressing of pebbles into sand, the grating against a leather sole, brought his head round with a jerk. A slow, sincere smile spread across his lean face.

"Epps, my man, where the deuce have you been?" His tone belied his growing frustration, but his man was not fooled.

Epps gave him a quick once-over and grunted. The viscount was not faring well cooped up all day, every day. Not even his nightly excursions were serving to assuage that restless spirit.

"Dinna ye think Epps would leave ye be more 'n a day, m'lord! They been watching me too close these days and I've had to stay quiet." He shoved the bundle under his arm forward and waited for his master to take it up. "Thought ye might be needing these, seeing as ye can't be doing laundry 'ere."

"Thank you, Epps." The viscount jumped off his rock

40

and took up the bundle of clothing and food and walked with his man toward a destination. "Midnight is low on feed..."

"Aye, thought as much. That's why tomorrow afternoon I'll be going into town to pick up a load...some of which will fall off m'cart...not far from 'ere." He rubbed his chin. "I'd bring it meself to the cliffs, m'lord, but fer fear someone might note it."

The viscount patted his back. "No, Epps...just leave it on the moors. I'll find it." He sighed long. "'Tis about time I came out of hiding and attended to my affairs in proper fashion."

"No, m'lord. Ye canna niver do that! Why...ye'd be hanging yerself and the proud Montlaine name!" cried Epps in some distress.

"And how am I to clear it trussed up...here?" They had by now reached the opening of a long wide cave. Within were artifacts of the viscount's stay, and to one side a stall of sorts had been erected for Midnight.

"Ain't Mr. Parks coome up with nuthin' yet?"

"My friend Mr. Parks has been doing all he can just to stall off the legal transfer of the estate to my cousin."

"Whot 'e should be doing is talking to poor Melony's friends...aye...jest whot I been doing meself!"

"Have you, Epps? My God, but there is no end to your abilities. And what have you come up with?"

"This...though in truth I don't know how it can help. The wench was wit' child...and she niver told no one it was yers! No...fact is...'ave it that ye...begging yer pardon, m'lord, weren't the light in 'er eyes!"

"Well, well...and who was it that stole her heart from me?" the viscount asked, his voice low, thoughtful.

"Don't know. No one seems to know...though she used to meet him at night. Her mother...she thought 'twas you...and when she found yer piece of glitter in her hand that night..."

"And I would be the one who would stop in the light of day to praise the poor child. But Epps, there is more to it than that ... much more, for she was not the only girl leaving her cottage at night, dressed in those odd hooded garments."

Epps sighed, for this was beyond his ken. "Sad is to say that is a truth ... and all of 'em daughters of neighboring tenants ... none yer own."

"Yes, and only neighboring tenants had problems with their cattle ... our tenants never seemed affected by the strange illnesses that befell the others."

"And ye wit' yer eyebrows ... and cooming from the war wit' not a scratch on ye, well, superstitious folk will go on aboot sech things," put in Epps.

The viscount grinned. "Such is my fate, but off with you now before you are missed at the house, and in future, Epps, I think we should limit our visits to the tunnel as we have in the past."

"Aye, but this time I won't be missed, m'lord. Them Echworths are up to Penrod ... looking after Miss Mary."

"Are they, by God? They'll not have her, Epps. I'll come out of hiding before I will allow that."

"Aye, so I thought, but m'people tell me Penrod hides her well, though the child grieves for ye. She coomes up here to Bodmin and it sore muddles m'head when I think on it. Might be right if I was to drop a hint that ye be alive."

"Not yet, Epps. She is a child, and if she knows I am well she will want to see me, bring me things. It would end in trouble."

"Aye, och ... these are sad days at Montlaine!"

"They are no better at Bodmin Heights," the viscount laughed.

The wind played with Vanessa's auburn curls beneath her blue riding hat. Above and in the west the sun was setting, putting an end to a clear crisp summer's day. Vanessa laughed and squeezed her calves into her horse's flanks, keeping the mare in an extended canter as they took the dirt road. At her back rode her brother and cousin. Ahead of them lay Montlaine, eerie in its gray jutting form, irregular, stark and totally magnificent against a darkening sky.

"Ho there, Shadow!" she called as she reined in to await the progress of her companions.

Her brother drew up alongside and complained, "Confound it, girl! Must you run neck or nothing?"

She smiled. "I daresay you and Randy are done in by now, but need I remind you that *I* was cooped up nearly all day with Guss, letter writing and then with Guss's dowager luncheon guest?" She pulled a grimace. "Dull sport, I do assure you!"

Randy arrived in time to hear this last and shook his head sympathetically. "I was never so glad to escape anything in all my life. Good Lord, what a bore! Didn't want to leave you, Ness, but couldn't very well take you to a cockfight, now could we?"

She sighed. "No, I don't suppose you could, but how the deuce you managed to find one after being in the neighborhood less than two days is beyond me!" She let go a soft laugh. "But never mind, it was an excellent notion of yours to call on the Echworths for tea. I must admit to a certain curiosity about them . . . and Montlaine." She turned her attention to the high-rising castle in the distance.

"Now, Nessie . . ." began her brother on a worried note.

"Well, aren't you curious, Rick? I mean . . . 'tis all so

43

strange! What of the missing Montlaine child, Mary ... and the girl I saw in the woods at Penrod? Why wouldn't Auntie Guss answer any questions about her after the Echworths left yesterday evening? Why all the mystery?"

"I don't know ... and Ness, 'tis none of our affair," returned her brother.

She said nothing to this but smiled to herself and clicked her horse into action. They took the road in easy time, and before long the heavy studded doors of Montlaine were opening to take them in.

A tall, lean and rigid-looking butler led them to the library, where he bade them be comfortable while he went in search of Mrs. Echworth. Lady Vanessa scanned the room. In spite of its enormous size, its furnishings gave it the appearance of warmth. The walls were lined for the most part with shelves upon shelves of books, but its most captivating feature was a full-length portrait above the fireplace. Vanessa went to it and made a low exclamation. A man, hatless, black hair tousled by the winds, black cape blowing, white shirt untied to the waist, astride a black stallion rearing, snorting and pawing the air. A chill went through her entire body as she studied the painting. Yet she could not tear herself away from it. It arrested her very soul, and she found herself studying the man's face. Black satanic brows above black forceful eyes. A leanness to the hard face, harder jaw. All she could think was, who was he? Surely a fictional subject?

So engrossed with the portrait was she that she felt a twinge of irritation when the three Echworths entered the scene and she was forced into the circle of greetings. Leaving Sheila and her mother to the lively

44

banter of brother and cousin, she turned her attention once again to the portrait.

Orson Echworth moved away from the friendly group gathered around the tea tray and studied Lady Vanessa. Her blue riding habit suited her lovely form. Her auburn curls clustered about her face and neck. Her cheekbones were high and well defined, and her eyes . . . those glittering silver jewels could do a man in if they wanted. It was strangely provoking to find that even in his death, Montlaine could snare a wench's glance!

"Ah . . . I see my late cousin holds your attention." He stood very near to her.

Vanessa turned to find his attractive face close, very close to her own. She took a step backward but relieved the moment with a warm smile. "He is an imposing subject . . . but you called him your cousin?" Her brow went up. There was certainly no family likeness.

He conceded this with a rueful grin. "My mother and his father were cousins. We were never much alike."

She was puzzled. The painting was that of a young man . . . not quite thirty. How had he died? "I suppose the painting was done in his heyday?"

"It was done less than a year ago . . . by the great Lawrence himself. I find it a bit distasteful myself."

She was surprised. "Distasteful? But . . . why?" There was something in all this she was not sure she understood. Something below the surface, and it made her uneasy.

"The pose he takes on that frothing black animal . . . look at them! They appear to rage against the heavens! With all that he had, he was never contented . . . even on canvas. It was no wonder it would end in his being called the devil."

45

It wasn't right, speaking about someone she had never known in this manner. She smiled diplomatically, wanting to know more, wishing to learn more, yet wanting it to take on a different hue. "And now...your cousin is gone...and so young." It was softly said.

Echworth shot her a quick glance. There was a depth to his chit. He felt himself on the defensive. He wanted to show her that if he spoke harshly of the late viscount, it was with cause. "Yes, he is gone...he died dragging himself and the Montlaine name through the mud!"

"Did he? I am sorry to hear it. Perhaps..."

"You mean to find an excuse for him?" He shook his head. "I would rather by far there was one...but I am afraid he brought about his own destruction."

"I see." The late viscount's death seemed shrouded in mystery. She thought about all the scrapes she had been through herself. It was always so easy for people to judge, but she knew from personal experience there were no absolutes.

Echworth glanced at his mother. That worthy woman was happily promoting her daughter to the two eligible bachelors she found in her web. He led Vanessa to a chair, took one up beside her and sighed as he began, "I am afraid it is not a pretty tale, my dear."

"I thought not. If it were, there would be no mystery."

"To understand the incidents that led to his death, you must realize that my late cousin was a hard-living man whose boredom with everyday reality led him to pursue a dangerous...imprudent course."

"He was, I take it, something of a libertine." She was smiling strangely.

He glanced at her countenance and wondered what it was she was thinking, wondered why it was she was

46

not shocked. After all, most young maids her age would have already been blushing at the insinuations. Lady Vanessa seemed only tolerantly amused!

"Precisely so. He began exploring the pleasures of the outer limits... it ended with the villagers suspecting him of practicing witchcraft... sorcery."

Her delicate brow arched. "A fact... or a fantasy, Mr. Echworth?"

"I was never sure... he would only laugh when I mentioned the matter to him."

"I see... and so the villagers suspected the viscount of Montlaine of practicing witchcraft. Why?"

"Scattered incidents... it would be gossip to go into them now. Suffice it to say that a young girl... a farmer's child who had often been seen in his company... died under mysterious circumstances, clutching the viscount's pendant... a pendant, I might add, that is a round onyx stone with Lucifer's sign emblazoned upon it."

"Oh, but this is all ludicrous. What nonsense ... witchcraft in this day and age!"

"Perhaps. At any rate, a warrant was issued and the magistrate with his deputies, and a good round of outraged villagers, came up to Montlaine one evening some four weeks ago. Montlaine would not be taken in. They chased him over the moors to Bodmin Heights... a mistake on his part, for the cliffs were at his back and there was no where to run."

"A mistake? How could a man make such a mistake?"

"Perhaps he was foxed. At any rate, he jumped off his horse and the animal took off for home. I wasn't there but I was told how he then backed up... slipped... and fell to his death."

She opened her mouth and then closed it. Something

47

inside of her rejected this story. It was all wrong. It didn't jive with the sensitivity in the face of the man in the painting. It was no fit ending for such a man. "And his sister, Mary . . . the girl you came to Penrod looking for?"

"The odd thing is that she vanished on the same night,"

"Why?" She was puzzled by all this. There was a piece missing to this story. A very important piece.

He shrugged. "We won't know that until we find her."

She sighed. "A very violent tale. . . . Does the black stallion pine for his master?"

"Another oddity. The stallion broke down his stall some days after the viscount fell to his death. Epps, the viscount's man, tried finding the horse for days . . . but he too has simply vanished."

It was at this moment that Sheila broke in and Echworth realized that everyone had been listening to his narrative. "The horrid thing about it now is that the servants are saying the viscount's ghost has taken Midnight into some nether region and that they ride the moors at night!" She shivered and found Richard's hand patting her own.

"But Orson, dear, this is not the sort of thing to be burdening our guests with." There was a hint of anger in his mother's tone.

A clock chimed and Vanessa rose hastily, sparing Mr. Echworth a reply. "Oh dear . . . time has flown. What an agreeable hour we have spent."

"Please, Lady Vanessa . . . do stay on to dinner," cordially urged Mrs. Echworth.

"I am very sorry, Mrs. Echworth, as much as we should all like to do that, we are promised to dine with

Lady Penrod this evening, and as she keeps country hours we had better be on our way."

Richard of Grey turned desperately to his latest heartthrob. "Miss Sheila... please do come to dinner..."

"What an excellent notion!" put in Randy, much in earnest over the same flower.

"That is very sweet of you both... but I don't know if I should. 'Tis such short notice for Lady Penrod..."

"But Guss will be delighted... won't she, Ness?" This from Ricky to his sister.

Something told Vanessa that this was not so, but she smiled politely. "I am sure her ladyship would be most happy to have you."

"You see!" Randy appeared tottering on the edge of abject joy. "You cannot refuse us now."

"But... it is still to Orson to decide, for he shall have to fetch me home."

"I am dreadfully sorry to disoblige you, Sheila, but I am promised to friends this evening."

"It doesn't signify!" returned Richard of Grey. "*We* shall be more than happy to see Miss Sheila safely home."

"Well then, Mama...?"

Mrs. Echworth scarcely concealed her bliss. "I certainly don't want to put a damper on your spirits. If Lady Vanessa is certain..."

Lady Vanessa nodded that she was and thus found herself following a lively group out of Montlaine. They had not progressed very far on horseback before Lady Vanessa made up her mind that the pretty Sheila was empty-headed and somewhat ill-mannered. How it was that her dearest and closest male relatives escaped this observation was beyond her patience, and she began to fall back from the happy trio. Besides, there was something on her mind, something that needed exploring.

"Go on ahead, Rick...I've dropped my scarf and shall catch up to you presently."

"Forget the scarf, Ness," objected her brother. "It's growing dark..."

"Tish! Forget my good silk scarf? Don't worry...I shan't be long." She smiled and waited for them to round the bend in the road. Yes, it was dark...probably far too dark for her to be undertaking such an adventure, but she had an overwhelming desire to see Bodmin Heights! Bodmin Heights...and it was only just across the moors!

Chapter Five

The viscount led his horse down the beach and away from the boulders that concealed the mouth to his cave dwelling. Above him, stars twinkled and a moon, half shadowed by passing clouds. It had been a long hard day drenched in boredom, and he looked forward to his projected outing. He had to visit with Parks, one of the few men alive who knew how things stood with him. He knew only one thing: he had not caused Melony's strange death, and therefore someone else had. There was only one way to clear the name of Montlaine, and he wasn't any closer to that than he had been four weeks ago!

Down the narrow stretch of pebbly beach he led his horse past the overhanging cliffs of Bodmin to an incline whose winding path led to the moors above. He looked up before mounting his horse and sighed. This was always the dangerous part of his excursions. However, there was nothing for it, and he put his horse into an extended trot and weaved round jutting rocks and smooth egg-shaped boulders. All seemed at peace across the moors. A gentle sea breeze took the heather shoots and shifted their weight. Wildflowers mingled with salt air and gave off a pungent and not unpleasant aroma.

Quietly he urged his horse forward and sought out the satchel of grain that Epps had promised to leave for him. This was found in a trice and secured to the back of his flat leather saddle. However, he had no sooner remounted his steed than the animal snorted and pawed the earth.

The viscount frowned and looked about to find riding toward him a stranger! From the seat, he would have thought the rider a lad, but from the form, he knew it to be a woman riding astride, and what was worse . . . she had seen him! Away! There was scarcely a moment to get out of sight! But Midnight, charged with his master's anxiety, reared high and in his frenzy the stallion blew out air, hoofing at the sky all the while.

Vanessa had been on the verge of turning back. Night had come on her suddenly, and the moors took on a frightening hue. However, something caught her eye. She trotted her horse deeper into Bodmin Moors and saw the form of a dark horse and rider, and suddenly both were in the air. Had she allowed her imagination to run amok she might have thought the sound she heard a devil's laughter. Instead, she didn't allow herself to think. She held herself and her horse in check. Shadow's ears were high, her neck tucked, her legs ready to run in the opposite direction, for she could feel her mistress's legs tremble, and that was a sure warning that all was not well.

The dark rider went onto his stallion's neck and the horse came down and bolted straightaway. A black cape flapped wildly in the wind, and suddenly both horse and rider were gone!

Vanessa held her horse still in check. A ghost? Had she seen the ghost of Montlaine? The horse had been real...hadn't he? This was impossible. She did not believe in devils, witches and ghosts! This was wrong...all wrong. Go home. A cautious voice within strongly urged, go home. Danger! Danger! Danger! The warning flickered before her eyes. But an even stronger voice scoffed and returned an answer, *investigate!*

So it was that lady Vanessa of the house of Grey proceeded to follow the vanishing night rider. She reached the approximate area where she had last seen the duo and nimbly jumped off her horse. The ground was hard and it was too dark to see if the questionable vision had left prints. Shadow nudged her back, and she nearly jumped with fright. With a hand to her heart she admonished severely, "Don't do that, love!" She took the reins. "Now...come along with me...quietly."

She led the mare to a cluster of gigantic granite rocks and discovered there a mazelike path that led sharply downward to the sea. Hesitantly she walked her mare down the sandy, narrow path, between rocks and low shrubbery. She could hear the breaking surf scraping the pebble beach, and then suddenly the boulders spread apart and she found herself staring at a narrow stretch of beach, most of which lay beneath the overhanging cliffs of Bodmin Heights.

Instinct told her to stop. It was enough. Curiosity moved her forward. Recent horse droppings told her she was on the correct trail. Anticipation filled her with excitement. It was as though everything that made her what she was had come into play for this one event.

There was no time to think. The viscount stalled his horse in the darkness of his makeshift habitat and rushed out to discern how far the unknown rider had followed him. He heard the sound of Vanessa's mare as the animal snorted against the salt spray of the crashing breakers. A prodigious female this, to follow him alone, at night, into such depths. Who could she be? With any luck she would not discover the mouth of the cave. Its natural concealment was such that it was not readily visible.

He backed away and used a rock formation as cover while the lady led her mare on. As she passed he got a glimpse of her profile and thought surely the moonlight played tricks with his vision. No maid, so young, so fair, could be on such a dangerous lark at this hour.

There was only beach and rocks ahead. The cliffs curved at the end of the beach and stretched out into the ocean. There was no escape for the night rider beyond. She turned around. At her back a similar landscape. An answer? She turned to study the fifty-foot wall of granite that loomed at her side and shaded the sand she stood upon. No ascent there. It was both steep and smooth...standing at a right angle with the beach. Where then?

Rock formations stood like eerie beings from another dimension. They created nooks and crevices. Perhaps he and his horse were lying in wait behind one or more of these? She weaved among these. Forgotten were her brother, cousin, Sheila and dinner at Lady Penrod's. Determinaton moved her now. Her arm brushed up against dried shrubbery, and she pushed at it and as she did so, it gave way. Vanessa stopped. Her lips parted but she made no sound. Her heart quickened but she took no step. There, right before her eyes, was the mouth of a cave. Forbidding in its blackness. Unwelcoming, threatening and ineffably irresistible.

She sucked in air, bolstered herself, wished for a light and promptly rubbed shoulders with a lantern and a long-stemmed match. She lit it, wrinkled her nose at the odor and held it up high. Within, quiet now, no longer appearing to be snorting fire, was Midnight in what seemed a fair enough stall. He was saddled still, and there was sweat glistening on his neck.

She moved inside and went to him. The mare cautiously allowed the stallion to rub her nose, and in spite of her fears Vanessa gave a short amused laugh. She hooked the reins of her mare around one stirrup and let her be as she went deeper into the cavern to discover a straw bed, several books and many artifacts indicating a male boarder was in residence.

"Humble ... but I call it home." The voice was deep, self-assured and slightly sardonic.

Vanessa whirled around. 'Twas the viscount of Montlaine. Here was the portrait come to life. Here was the libertine, the suspected murderer. What could she say? Manners and breeding came to her rescue and restored her voice. "I ... I am sorry ... truly. I know I have stumbled upon something you have been at pains to keep hidden ... but when I saw what rumor has called a ghost, I could not credit it. You see, I don't believe in ghosts."

Her response, like everything she had done this evening, surprised him. He was intrigued. He took a step forward. "You don't believe in ghosts?" His black eyes surveyed her dubiously. "What then did you think you would find?"

"An explanation." She didn't mean to be profound, but it was all she could say beneath his glance. His eyes penetrated, mesmerized, vaguely thrilled her.

His satanic brow moved. "So you came sleuthing? With no concern for your safety?" His tone was contemptuous.

"Am I in danger, sir?"

He laughed ruefully. "You might very well be, if all they say about me is true." There was a tinge of bitterness in his voice.

"So then ... you *are* the viscount of Montlaine?"

He made her a mock bow. "Since I am the only ghost that rides Bodmin Moors, you must have realized that."

"Actually ... I knew it from your portrait ... the one in the library of Montlaine."

Was there no end to the surprises this chit had in store for him? "Really? And are my cousins already entertaining in my home? How quickly they have put off their mourning clothes." Again the sarcasm.

She studied him a moment before replying, and then it was to avoid his comment by putting a question to him. "Why do you stay here? Why not leave the country? You could then establish yourself elsewhere ... in exile, of course, but with your wealth still in your control."

This was preposterous. Here he was talking to this perfect stranger about matters that were none of her concern. It enraged him to be in such a bind. He turned away from her and paced.

She waited only a moment and called his attention. "I have offended you with my blunt speaking. I am sorry for it, as it is obvious you find your situation ... embarrassing."

He rounded on her. "Embarrassing? My pretty little sleuth, you have no notion of what you are speaking. I am suspected of witchcraft most vile ... of creating a coven of twelve girls, of deflowering them ... using them in hoary orgies ... causing the death of one in particular. I am called Lucifer, the demon of lechery!"

"And still you remain ... existing in this cave ... to what end?"

He glanced at her sharply. "I remain because I want

56

to clear my name ... for the sake of Montlaine ... for the sake of my young sister, Mary."

"I know." She smiled and was pleased to see the hint of an answering smile in his own black eyes.

His brows frowned, his lashes flickered. "Who are you?"

"I am Lady Vanessa of the house of Grey. I am here at Penrod with my cousin and brother."

"And had the misfortune of following me," he interrupted her.

She inclined her head. "If you think so. However, the question now remains, what do you propose to do ... about me?" She was all too aware of the fact that he had stood blocking the exit during their entire discussion. He was a desperate man and as such he might not think it unreasonable to keep her a prisoner here and thus protect himself.

"What to do? You say your brother and cousin are with you at Penrod? Will not Lady Penrod soon send them off in search of you?"

"Most certainly ... but I don't suppose they will come in this direction."

"Aha, then you admit to being at my mercy?"

She moved as though to pass him, saying unwisely, "Not in the least, my lord!"

The action provoked him. He took up her shoulders and forced her around. "You are vastly mistaken, little sleuth. I have too much at stake to let you go jauntering out of here with the best jest ever to go round a tea party!" His eyes were smoldering, for her own glittering gray jewels excited him. "I could if I wished, keep you here ... indefinitely."

"You wouldn't dare!" She was angry now. She was unused to his offhanded manner. Men usually paid her court in high style.

"Haven't you heard the demon Montlaine would dare anything? Is it not what even his own cousins are whispering?"

"I have also heard Montlaine himself say he wished to clear his name," she returned quietly.

He dropped his hands. "You had better go . . . your brother and cousin will be worried."

She hesitated. "You haven't asked me to keep your secret."

He laughed harshly. "A promise extracted from a woman is a meaningless bauble."

She frowned. "I mean to prove you wrong, my lord." She moved to her mare, took up the reins and turned back to find him staring after her. "Your secret is safe with me. Goodnight, my lord."

For a long while after she had gone, the viscount of Montlaine stared after her. At last and after much pondering, he chose to leave his fate, for the moment, in her hands. He took up his horse and once again attempted the trip across the moors to his friend and counsel, Mr. Parks.

Chapter Six

In the distance, candlelights glowed in the windows of a small but attractive two-story cottage. High evergreens swayed at its back, sloping off into a valley of woods rich and green. A welcome sight, and the viscount of Montlaine breathed a sigh of relief.

His counselor and friend Edward Parks lived some ten miles north of Wadbridge village, a circumstance that the viscount had thanked the fates for several times in the past four weeks.

Up the winding drive to the neat stables. Jerry, the one groom Parks maintained, stuck out his head from the loft window and called, "Coo there, m'lord . . . I'll be down . . ."

The viscount dismounted and held out the reins to the shuffling older man. "Jerry . . . he needs a rubdown. I think he is blowing some."

The groom held his weathered hand to the stallion's nose.

"Aye, that he is. Don't ye worrit none, m'lord . . . I'll walk 'im and see 'e eats no grain till 'e cools off."

"Thank you, Jerry . . . and mind, now, put him in the far stall . . . though I don't think you are expecting anyone else?"

"No . . . 'e'll be safe enough wit' me."

For the man's trouble the viscount slipped him a coin and proceeded on his way to the cottage. After a momentary wait a round pleasant-faced woman with a bob of unruly steel-gray curls beneath a mop cap appeared. She pressed her hands together with a show of genuine delight.

"M'lord . . . it's that pleased I am to see ye . . . but och now, ye been losing weight . . . and no wonder . . . but go on, he'll be waiting on ye in the library and I'll be fetching ye a proper meal!"

"Thank you, Matty . . . but don't go to any trouble. It's late and I'm certain you want your rest."

She waved such a consideration aside. "Trouble indeed. 'Tis me honest pleasure to set a tray for ye, m'lord."

He gave her a warm smile and moved across the narrow hall to an undersized dark oak door. Parks's servants were few and totally trustworthy. He had little to worry about when he was under this roof.

Edward Parks was standing by the fire, rereading a letter he had received from a friend in London. The sound of the opening door brought his head up, and his lips twitched appreciatively as the viscount entered.

"By Jupiter, man, if you don't look the devil! Why do you insist in going about in black?"

"Good evening to you, you old dog!" He went forward and gave his friend a hearty shoulder shake. "And I go about in black because it blends in with the night. Now, what news have you for me?"

Edward Parks ran his hand through his sandy hair and sighed. "Not very much, Bret. Your cousin Duncan remains in London, an odd circumstance considering he stands to inherit."

"But he cannot inherit, can he? Not without a body . . . or the passage of some defined time. Why should he come to Montlaine now? It might only appear suspicious."

"Yes, but . . . you say suspicious . . . the sorry truth is Duncan was the only one who stood to gain by your destruction, and *he was in London!*"

"Was he, Edward? Or did he just appear to be?"

"He was in London . . . as far as I can ascertain. I have just received a letter today from Lady Jersey in answer to the query I put to her. He was often seen in London these last six months. 'Tis no little journey to and fro from Montlaine."

Montlaine sighed wearily and took up an upholstered wing chair, putting up his booted feet on the coffee table. "What then? Do I give myself up and hope for the best?"

"Indeed you do not!" returned his friend adamantly. "Good Lord, Bret, we know one of those damned Echworths was behind it all. We simply must find out who."

"And then prove it. My naive Edward . . . the people want me as their villain. I look the part. They are not going to settle for a fair Echworth easily."

"I think, Bret, that we have been going about this all wrong. What we need is a new plan of action," said Parks thoughtfully.

Montlaine smiled as though he were discussing another's fate and not his own. "Yes, well, never mind that now, Edward. I have a new problem to put before you."

"Oh? And pray how did you manage to dig up more trouble, secluded as you are?"

"I was on my way to you tonight, not far from the

cave, when I was seen. She followed..."

"She? You say you were followed by a woman?" Parks was incredulous.

"Precisely. She tracked me to earth and then gave her promise freely not to divulge my little secret."

"But... who is she?"

"Lady Vanessa of Grey." Montlaine was frowning as he said the name. It had been bothering him ever since the beauty had given it to him.

"Upon my life! Bret... never say you have tangled with *Naughty Lady Ness?*" expostulated Parks. His pale-blue eyes were quite round with his amazement.

Montlaine slapped his knee. "Damn! So that is who she is. I have been racking my brain trying to think why the name rang a bell. Well, well, Naughty Lady Ness. I have heard any number of tales about the chit." He smiled to himself, remembering her face, her voice, her audaciousness. "I can see now there must have been a great deal of truth to what they say about the lady."

"What they say about the lady is that she is up to every rig! A jester, a high flyer, and the last I heard she was organizing a cricket match... eleven ladies against eleven males... and Bret, the ladies took it!"

"And what is a lady of her tastes doing here in quiet Cornwall?" mused Bret.

"I don't know. Probably got herself caught up in a scrape her parents couldn't hush up. Sent her off till the hum quiets. Unconventional, that one, but I like her and think she can be trusted."

This time Bret's eyes rounded. "You know her?"

"As to that... no, I don't, but I saw her on one occasion. It was during one of her scrapes in fact. Some boor had the crudeness to take a stick to his old dog on a public street. Lady Vanessa was passing by in her phaeton. I became aware of the scene suddenly, for I was standing not far off. Apparently she jumped down from her carriage, put the reins in her tiger's hands, pulled a young man, whom I ascertained later was her brother, along with her across the street and rounded on the man in time to wrench the stick out of his hands and swat him on the shoulder with it!"

"Good Lord . . . a veritable tigress!" the viscount laughed.

"You may remark upon it. The dog was naught but a mongrel, but as the churlish individual jumps back in shock, she bends to pick the dirty creature up in her hands." He shook his head over the memory. "She throws a coin at the man's feet and starts off with the dog . . . but the brute dared to hold her arm."

The viscount frowned. "Devil you say!"

"Precisely. It was then I moved forward to intervene, but there was no need, for her brother brings up his fives and lands the chap a settler." He smiled. "What a row they left behind."

"And the Naughty Lady?"

"She thanked her brother for knocking the nasty man down . . . her words exactly . . . and off they went, leaving yet another set-to at their backs."

Bret let go a laugh. It was a course that released much pent-up tension. At last he lay back in his chair and sighed contentedly.

"And from that incident you surmise that the lady is to be trusted?"

"I do," replied Parks hestitantly.

"The wonder is that I never ran into the vixen during my London days last year."

"As to that, Bret . . . you *were* floating in rather dubious circles, gaming in the worst of hells and avoiding Almack's at all costs."

"Almack's ... hmmm ... I did manage to keep it at arm's length." He turned, for the door had opened to emit Matty laden with a tray.

He then proceeded to eat his dinner with some relish, and when his friend suggested that he stay the night and return to his cave in the dusk of the following day he was quick to agree. He wanted a decent bath and a comfortable bed, and with Naughty Lady Ness now holding his fate in her active little hands he was as safe at Parks's cottage as he might be in his cave.

Gloomy shadows. Indistinct figures, hooded all, waving dark pendants and beckoning. Vanessa felt herself slipping into their circumference, and then blood-red eyes glared wrathfully. She groaned and protested their onslaught, for they were reaching for her, touching her, and their touch was cold and repelling. And then they all stopped to look up as a voice took command. A strangely familiar, not unwelcome voice, and the features of Montlaine glistened above the branch of candles. "Move aside!" he demanded. "She is Lucifer's prize!"

Vanessa couldn't bear it and with a jerk she awoke and sat bolt upright in her bed. She shook off the remains of her sleep. Dreadful! She had been traveling from one nightmare into another, and all centered around Montlaine! Guilty or not guilty?

She couldn't have thought so when she gave her promise to keep his secret ... but now? She wasn't sure. A suspicion crept up. It was possible that his pride, his vanity, had kept him in the depths of Bodmin. He could be guilty ... but looking for a way out, looking for a trick to prove himself innocent? He was an arrogant man ... strong-willed ... with a dangerous temper. She had felt some of this when he had dared to take hold

64

of her shoulders and claim his power over her. Yet he had let her go. Oh! What was this man of Montlaine?

She remembered her sensations as she rode over the moors back toward the main pike and Penrod. Excitement overriding all, and something else she could not put a name to, did not want to think about. But how angry Rick had been. He had come charging at her alone, furious because he had reluctantly allowed his cousin to escort Sheila to Penrod, while he returned in search of Vanessa.

She had put him off easily, saying that she had lost her way in the dark, and then she admonished him not to stand about brandishing words when they should hasten their pace to Penrod. It wasn't long before she had picked up his humor, and the evening had passed tolerably well. Randy and Rick, steadfast friends always, were beginning to eye each other askance, for both vied for Miss Sheila's notice. Vanessa disliked the girl, writing her off as shallow, but she wasn't yet too concerned about her brother's involvement in that direction.

Instead she turned her attention to Lady Penrod, quietly taking her aside. "Guss? Do be truthful and tell me ... what have you done with Mary of Montlaine? Is she stuffed into the attic, forced to take meals alone, living a hermit's life? And if so ... why?"

Lady Penrod studied her young guest penetratingly. "What a very odd thing to suggest."

"Is it so odd? Oh, Guss ... stranger things are happening in Cornwall ... aren't they?" She put up a finger. "Please, Guss ... in confidence, between us, what of the child?"

Guss sighed. She turned her head to glance at Sheila, and then, satisfied that the chit was fully occupied with her admirers, she pleated the silk of her mauve gown before bringing her glance once more to Vanessa's face. She opened her mouth as though to speak and then her winged brows arched expressively. "Ness...this is more than a confidence...this is a matter of the child's life."

"Is it? Why?"

"Ness...dear...I knew the late viscount...knew him well...how can I tell you? He was wild as a youth...unhappy in many things, discontent...he went off to fight the French in Spain...did well for himself, he and his man Epps...but they came back last year at the end of '14, and Bret was idle again. Some of his time he spent in the gaming hells of London...some of it in worse establishments than either of us are supposed to know exist. He gained for himself a reputation, and it haunted him to Montlaine." She took a long gulp of air. "Six months ago he returned to Montlaine. Tenants were complaining...the lands needed management...and it presented a challenge to Bret. Within a short span of time he began to work wonders and his tenants thrived. However, he had had some words with neighboring farmers, I forget why and it doesn't really matter...what does is that in anger he cursed them...verbally, you understand...but within days, their sheep fell ill!"

"This is preposterous. You are telling me..." started Ness.

"No, I am not telling you anything but what happened to make the villagers wary of him. Then rumors started that some of the village girls—merchants' daughters, tradesmen's daughters and farmers' daughters—were going out late at night dressed in black hooded robes. Where they went, no one knew; who they met, no one knew. But everyone suspected Montlaine."

"Why?"

"Because of the pendant he wore... because many of the girls were seen flirting with him. He was a ladies' man you know."

"This pendant... what should make it suspicious?"

"I begged him to put it off... but he had sentimental reasons and a certain obstinacy as well. It had been given to him in Spain by a professor of sorts... he held the man dear..."

"But what was it about the pendant that made the villagers suspect him of being in league with the devil?"

"It was emblazoned with Lucifer's mark... at least, the vicar had remarked upon it one day in passing. But Bret would only laugh at such things."

"I see. Now... what of Mary? Why is she in danger... and from whom, the villagers?"

"You see, it might be thought that as his sister, she was a part of his coven. They know only that twelve girls were needed for the coven; it still isn't known exactly who those twelve girls were. They might try to harm her... but I doubt that very much. Personally, I think she is more in danger of being taken advantage of by the Echworths... though I don't know how much longer I can hold them at bay. They are her legal guardians now."

Vanessa's finger moved across her cherry lips as she organized her thoughts. "Who stood to gain by the viscount's destruction?"

"You say destruction... not death?"

"If someone planned and schemed and came up with this bizarre framework to trap the late viscount, they couldn't be certain he would be killed... but he would be destroyed."

"The only man who stands to gain is Duncan... the eldest Echworth... and he was in London during the past six months!"

67

"A loving mother might go to some lengths to secure her son's future," suggested Vanessa archly.

Guss considered this with a tilt of her head and a frown. "She is, in her own way, quite a cunning woman. But Ness . . . there *was a man* among those twelve girls on their meetings in the moors."

"Was there?" Vanessa shifted in her chair. "How do we really know that? I mean you have only just finished telling me that no one knew anything very much about this dreadful organization."

"That is true, but we have it from the vicar that one of the thirteen was a man," returned Guss quietly.

"The vicar?"

"Indeed, Vicar Poole, you see, observed the cult on two different occasions."

"Never say so! Well then . . . what did he see?"

Augusta Penrod sighed heavily. "Not very much . . . though it was shortly after he discovered Melony's involvement with the cult that she was killed."

"Hold! You say he discovered her . . . this Melony? How so, Auntie Guss . . . how so?"

Lady Penrod eyed her young charge cautiously. "Now Vanessa dear, it is not all that interesting . . . you need not concern yourself."

"I shall explode!" exclaimed her guest. "Guss . . . do tell me at once. How did the Vicar discover Melony? How did he know one of the cult members was a man? How?"

"I am not quite certain how he knew, for I did not actually speak to him about the matter . . . but I did hear tell that he was the cause of the cult's dispersing, whereupon he chased after and caught Miss Fry!"

"Well, upon my soul!" She would have said more had Sheila not chosen that moment to join them. Thus, their discussion came to a close, and Lady Vanessa had retired with a muddle to pick her way through.

The night had seemed never-ending as she grappled with the mystery. She wanted the truth for the truth's sake. If Montlaine was innocent, he should be proved so, and if guilty, he should pay for his crime.

At last, sleep had enveloped her with its heaviness. Nightmares had taken over, one by one, until finally she awoke to the dawning of a new day. Through the open window the scent of Penrod roses cajoled her to her feet, but it was something else that set her pace at full speed. An idea had lodged itself neatly within her scope, and a pledged resolution set her goal within her grasp. She was certain the road was ahead—the only problem was in finding it!

Chapter Seven

The aroma of sweet rolls and hot coffee filled the dining parlor. A bright sun reflected the promise of a sweet summer's day. However, neither of these two advantages seemed to honey the tempers of Lord Richard of Grey and his cousin, Randall of Southvale.

They eyed one another across the breakfast table, waited only for the lackey to leave them to themselves before once again picking up the argument they had started the evening before.

"Don't think that because you choose to look the tulip in that waistcoat that Miss Echworth will pay you any more mind than she did last night!" grunted Ricky severely.

Randy pushed his plate away and stood up. "Tulip? Me . . . a tulip?" He paced and then rounded to stand before his cousin. "I say, Rick, that is coming on a bit too strong!" He blustered over this insult a moment and then found something he could throw at his cousin's head. "And I'll tell you what! I'd rather look a tulip in this waistcoat, which is you very well know all the crack, than appear a coxcomb in a cravat whose style went out with the diamond heelpiece!"

"*What?*" shrieked Rick, rising hastily to his feet and knocking down his chair. "Damn, but you've lost your senses boy!"

Randall put on an expression of disdain. However, this was unwise, for Richard of Grey took immediate umbrage and gave his cousin a hefty shove. Randy went backward with the force, caught his balance and put up his fives. The door to the dining room opened and in glided Lady Penrod, very much aware of what had been transpiring. However, to all outward appearances it was just another congenial morning.

"Ah ... you haven't started eating yet. How nice." She took up a seat at the table and motioned them with her eyes to attend her.

Their manners were not so forgotten that they would pursue an argument in her presence. Reluctantly and glaring at each other all the while, they followed suit and waited for Lady Penrod to carry the conversation.

"Wherever has Ness got herself this morning?" Lady Penrod dove right in.

"What? Is she not about then?" cried Vanessa's brother on a note of dismay.

"No." Lady Penrod was surprised at his concern. "What is it, Rick? Where has she gone?"

"Devil a bit, I don't know ..."

"Is there something wrong?" Lady Penrod was worried now.

"Yes, something is wrong!" wailed Randall of Southvale. "We were hoping Nessy would want to call on Miss Echworth this morning."

Lady Penrod's lips quivered, but she contained her amusement admirably. "Oh, I see." She considered the problem a moment and then offered, "There is, of course, no reason why you can't call on Miss Echworth yourselves."

"No...but we didn't want to appear to be too forward. After all, they are still in mourning," put in Ricky thoughtfully.

"Yes, it would be quite different if Ness were with us," added Randy.

"I see. Well then, you'll just have to put it off till tomorrow." Lady Penrod smiled.

Ricky and his cousin weren't pleased with this solution, and it was Ricky who ventured, "Well, but I don't see anything wrong in our calling...do you, Randy?"

"No, I don't suppose...though it would have been a dashed good treat to have been able to take Miss Echworth out for a drive. Do her some good to get out of that gloomy old castle for a bit."

"Ummm," agreed Ricky, his differences with his cousin momentarily put aside in the light of this new problem. "I don't think we had better suggest it to Mrs. Echworth now...it wouldn't be the thing, without Ness about to lend the scheme some propriety. Damnation! Where the deuce has that sister of mine taken herself off to this time?"

"Tell you what, Rick," suggested his cousin. "I'll lay you a monkey the chit is up to her old tricks again."

"Ho, Shadow...ho, mare," called Lady Vanessa sharply to her mount. The horse was fired up with the run they had had over the meadows. She reined in, however, under her mistress's capable hands and pawed the earth, impatient to be off again.

Vanessa leaned back in her flat saddle and adjusted her blue riding skirt about the horse. It wasn't seemly riding about the countryside astride and without a groom in attendance. As usual she hadn't thought the thing out, and it wasn't until now that it occurred to her that a vicar might raise an eyebrow at her unorthodox and somewhat hoydenish arrival on his scene. She surveyed the neatly laid out gray stone buildings ahead in the valley of the rolling downs, and her first reaction was one of consternation.

No flower beds, no shapely yews ornamented the bleak rough stone walls. There was life about in the dirt courtyard, for she could see a young maid scurry across dragging a milk bucket from a modest barnyard. There too, Vanessa could see chickens pecking in the dirt. Smoke twirled out of two chimneys, and still the entire package seemed unwelcoming. A tingle of dread shot through her. This vicar would be stern and rigid. He would not look upon her visit with pleasure. It was something she sensed. Nevertheless, she steeled herself and gently urged her horse to take the rolling downs at a decorous pace toward her objective.

Vicar Poole sat in his upholstered wing chair near the fire. The last log was burning to a close, and its embers were bright with the last of their fierceness. He brought his faded hazel eyes up from the contemplation of an essay by Alexander Pope, and studied the dying fire sadly. None would have guessed that Pope was a favorite of his, but then no one had ever really taken the trouble to know him. He sighed. Life had in many ways passed him by. He had never found the right woman to share his home, give him children. . . .

"'Scuse me, vicar . . ." It was Taby, his housekeeper, plump and well over fifty. She ran the household tightly and was the only servant whose respect for the vicar had not turned into fear.

"There be someone to see ye . . . a Lady Vanessa

74

Grey... waiting in the hall she is..."

The vicar's finely shaped brow went up with interest. "Really? I heard Lady Vanessa was up at Penrod. Whatever can she want here?" He stood up, and before the housekeeper could comment he waved her off. "Very well, show the young woman in... go on."

The housekeeper nodded and hands folded into one another at her waist she hurried off to do his bidding. A moment later Lady Vanessa was moving across the vicar's study and allowing him to take up her hand. She studied him as he bowed perfunctorily over her kid-gloved fingers and was surprised to find him a fairly young man. Not above five and thirty, she thought to herself, and if one looked past the stern thin lips, past the drawn cheeks, one might even find him attractive. However, he then brought up his eyes to her face, and Lady Vanessa was repulsed.

No, not attractive, not with those eyes. Here was a cold, self-righteous man. His voice belied this, for it came sweetly, gently. "Lady Vanessa, how may I serve you?" He offered her a chair.

She sat and spread her skirts demurely. "Shall I first pass the amenities, sir... or shall I get directly to the point that brings me here?"

He smiled, but he was not pleased with her manner. "By all means, my lady, do get to the point, as I am certain your time is valuable."

That is not what she meant. He knew it and she knew that he knew it, so she did not quibble to point it out. It was the sort of response she had expected. He was already living up to her estimate of his character. "Sir, it has come to my understanding that not very long ago the house of Montlaine suffered something of a tragedy. I am friend to Mrs. Echworth." She allowed herself a moment to swallow her white lie. "And would

75

for her sake do all I can to help in this matter."

He leaned toward her, his brows drawn together. Who the devil did she think she was? Come here to lord it over them? He found her gray eyes sparkling, her lips full with rosiness, her nose pert, her beauty alluring, and he tempered his response.

"My dear Lady Vanessa...I am certain you mean well, but what, may I ask, do you think you can do for the house of Montlaine?"

"I can do little. However, fortunately I am not alone in my desire to clear up the mystery that surrounds poor Mary of Montlaine and the Echworths. You see, both my brother and our cousin Randall of Southvale are with me at Penrod and hopeful that our combined efforts may prove beneficial in the matter."

He sighed. Damned interfering quality. Forever walking in and muddling up what was better left alone. "I still don't understand how any of you can help. The late viscount strayed from God! He took up the worship of Satan, seduced young maids to his wicked intent..."

"Hold just a moment!" Lady Vanessa felt her anger rising, though why it should, she told herself, was something very odd. "You are saying that the viscount of Montlaine engaged in demonology? You know this for a fact?"

He hesitated. It was what he had been saying. People had never before sought to question him in such doubting tones. It shook him with anger, but he was not so unwise as to show this. "I never saw the master leader's face. But the viscount made a mistake...the mistake of pride. He wore the symbol of Asmodeus around his neck."

"The pendant?"

"Yes."

"And because of that you believe him in league with the devil?"

"The symbol of Asmodeus...pertains to lechery. Asmodeus is the demon of lechery. The cult danced in a nine-foot circle, and their demon sign, scratched into the earth of that impious circle, was that of Asmodeus. So then, my lady, no, I did not in fact see the faces of those twelve girls...witches, servants of the devil! And no, I did not see the face of the thirteenth person at the head of their cult, but I saw his form. He had the height and breadth of an imposing male. I tell you it was a coven meeting I came across, not once, *but twice!* Each time there were twelve witches and one demon master!" His tone had risen with excitement. His eyes betrayed the quiet that his soul had never really achieved.

"But you did see one of these women...you did see Melony Fry?"

Vicar Poole's eyes went past Vanessa's countenance. Over her head he sent his gaze to the meadows beyond his doors. Melony's face blurred before him, evoking memories he wished in the grave with her. Melony. She had rejected him in every way. Melony, whom he had adored, wanted, cherished. So he had taken to watching her at her window at night. Not always, but now and then on his way home from the village. It was how he had come across the cult on that second fateful occasion.

He had followed Melony as she skulked out of her family's cottage and scurried across the fields. He had stood apart and watched in awe, thrilled, fired up and yet horrified, as the cult went through the sacrilege, the heretical whisperings. He had waited until he could stand no more and then he had burst in upon them. Away! How they had scattered away—but Melony could not escape him.

He had chased after her over the rolling downs. He had caught her and shaken her and shaken her till the tears were streaming over her white cheeks. He should have realized then . . . and now Melony was gone.

"Vicar . . . vicar?" It was Ness, her gaze penetrating his absorption with his memory, seeing there more than he would ever admit.

He shook himself from his daily nightmare and attempted to give her his attention. "Yes . . . I discovered Melony Fry and reported the incident to her parents. They promised to keep her indoors . . . but evidently the very next day she managed to get away for a few hours . . . just long enough for her demon master to poison her!"

Lady Vanessa sighed impatiently. She was getting nowhere with all this nonsense about demon masters. She needed facts! Well then, she would have to speak to someone whose life made her more realistic. Briskly she rose, and the vicar followed suit.

"Thank you, Vicar Poole. You have been most . . . patient." She smiled and moved toward the door, allowing him to see her down the corridor to the courtyard door. There she turned and extended her hand. "Don't trouble yourself further, sir. I shall fetch my horse myself and be off." Why did she feel as though she were escaping? He had no power over her. Why this sense of oppression?

He held her hand lingeringly, but there was disapproval in his glance. "Did you travel all the way from Penrod unaccompanied?"

"Alas, good sir, it won't help to scold me. I am set in my ways, and one of them is to jaunt about on my own." She bent and confided winningly, "You see, no groom could keep pace with me and my mare, Shadow."

He felt himself charmed by the light in her gray eyes, by the bounce of her auburn curls beneath the stylish blue riding hat, but he held himself in check. His lashes shaded his eyes. His mouth went sour. "Indeed, my lady, I am surprised at your brother and cousin. They should not let you go about alone. This is wild country, our Cornwall. Your city parks are nothing to the threat of our bogs and moors!"

She allowed him a throaty laugh. "Never fear, vicar, I watch for the red patches and make a wide circle round them. Bogs and moors are not unknown to me. My family seat is in the heart of Yorkshire." She waved herself off and moved toward the carriage house where her horse was being kept for her. She felt the vicar's eyes follow her and so was forced to go within. There she stopped and listened.

A young livery boy came forward and asked if she required her mare, but she held him off with her hand. "No . . . I think not yet. Tell me, lad, would the vicar's housekeeper be in the kitchen?"

"Taby? Aye . . . that she would, m'lady. Shall I fetch her to you?"

"No, I think I'll just go there myself."

"To the kitchen, m'lady?" The lad was dumbfounded by this announcement. Quality! Weren't they always about the oddest things? Forever breaking rules, even their own!

She smiled warmly, noting simultaneously that the vicar had at last withdrawn and closed the door at his back. "Why yes. I find I am a bit thirsty."

"Taby now, she'll be that surprised to 'ave ye drinking tea in her kitchen, but I'll take ye to 'er if ye 'ave a mind."

"You needn't bother about it. I shall find my own way. The kitchen is just around back, isn't it?"

He nodded and watched the pretty young woman go off. He scratched his head in puzzlement at such doings, shrugged it off and continued working at the wheels of the vicar's modest carriage.

Lady Vanessa found the kitchen door open. Nevertheless she knocked. A hearty voice called out a general welcome. "Aye, then . . . come in if ye will, me 'ands are that covered with flour and I can't be getting the door!"

"It's open, Taby . . . I hope you don't mind my coming around this way," ventured Lady Vanessa sweetly.

Taby turned her ruddy countenance and looked up to find Lady Vanessa descending upon her. She was surprised but knew well how to behave. The maid was up to something. She had sensed it the moment she had opened the front door to her earlier that morning, and here was her chance to discover what it was! She wiped her hands onto a dishrag, but the remains of her endeavors at strawberry pie were still smudged across her fingers and one red cheek.

"Och then . . . m'lady . . . come in, come in . . . though 'tis to the parlor I should be showing ye!"

Vanessa stepped into the cozy, antiquated kitchen and sighed. She was sick to death of always having to observe the proprieties. What was the difference if she spoke with a servant in the kitchen or in the parlor? And now especially when she didn't wish to be observed by the vicar. "Please don't concern yourself with my comfort. I shall do just fine." She crossed her arms over her middle. "I am not going to try to bamboozle you, Taby, and say that I've come for a spot of tea or a drink of water. You would see through it in a moment."

"Aye. There is no denying ye've come after something . . . but it ain't food nor drink, m'lady . . . meaning ye no disrespect," said the housekeeper cautiously.

"Very well then." She motioned for the housekeeper to take a chair and did the same. Putting her elbows on the small square table before her, she hesitated and then dove right into the meat of the matter. "I haven't been at Penrod long, as you probably have already heard, but nevertheless . . . I feel obligated to do something to unravel the tangle that affects our neighbors at Montlaine. I don't believe the truth was ever uncovered, and it should be. *You,* Taby, can help."

"Wisht now, how can I do that?"

"I didn't want to bother the vicar with further questions about Melony Fry ... he seemed rather vague in that quarter ..."

"Aye!" interrupted the housekeeper. "Ye did right there, m'lady. That's an open wound, it is. Bless him, he has had enough grief from that direction. Meaning no disrespect to the dead, but she were a little tart ... and as it turns out a heathen one as well!"

What did she mean? Was she saying that the vicar had been romantically interested in Melony Fry? She was excited with this piece of insight but she kept her exterior calm. "Are you saying that the vicar held Miss Fry in esteem?"

"I shouldn't be saying naught 'bout what the vicar felt or did," returned the housekeeper sharply.

"I am sorry. I didn't mean to meddle."

The housekeeper relented. "Ye don't want to be hearing 'bout that m'lady, and it won't help none."

"No, perhaps not. So then, Taby ... what *would* help is speaking to a girl who was in Miss Fry's confidence."

The housekeeper moved in her chair. Her face took on a thoughtful expression. "As it happens ... the magistrates inquired into the matter ... they didn't come up with no one. Not a girl would own to being Melony's friend."

Vanessa's face fell. "Surely she must have had one friend? She could not have been totally alone all through childhood ... one friend must have carried on?"

The housekeeper shuffled her feet. "Well ... it isn't common knowledge ... 'coz they kept it quiet and I

81

don't know that she'd own it now, seeing as Melony come to no good . . . but there was a slip of girl, daughter to old Widdons of Widdons's mill . . . just down the road. They thought no one saw 'em . . . but I would catch 'em holding their heads together in the back woods now and then. Often wondered if that Widdons girl was part of what the vicar saw," she mused.

Lady Vanessa nearly dropped her chair as she hastened to rise. This was beyond everything wonderful! This would answer. It had to. "Thank you, Taby. Thank you so much."

The older woman rose slowly to her feet and eyed Lady Vanessa speculatively. "Lookee, m'lady . . . meaning ye no disrespect, but it's over. He died . . . the viscount died and it all ended. Best leave it that way!"

"How can I, Taby? Mary of Montlaine lives. His memory lives. If they are innocent . . . should we allow them besmirched?"

Taby shook her ruddy cheeks. "'Tis a shame. He was ever a wild blade running amok over the fields. Spoiled he was . . . the only male child . . . his family proud . . . too proud. Often was the time he'd tease me with those black eyes . . . rough and tumble he was. But the devil's disciple? No . . . I would have swore he'd never go that route . . . still 'n' all . . ."

Lady Vanessa listened to this quietly. A vision of the viscount as a youth formed, and she became caught up with the fantasy. A mild regret that she had not known him then . . . shared their youth together . . . touched her, and then she was waving herself off, intent once more on her errand.

In a low-ceilinged tavern beneath sagging dark oak rafters, two gentlemen sat. Their appearance suggested that both were used to more elegant surroundings. Beaver top hats ornamented the small round table between them as they leaned into the shadows of their corner.

"Well, well, Mr. Parks," said Orson Echworth carefully, "it appears we shall come to terms, though I must admit, I am surprised."

"Are you? I can't imagine why," said Edward Parks casually.

"How shall I put this delicately?" Orson Echworth sighed, his fine brow twitching with his sneer. "I am afraid there isn't any way to put it that won't come out vulgar in the end. You are selling out, aren't you? Your late client and ... dear friend trusted you, and you are selling him short."

"He is gone and I am here and in debt. If I can be of some service to you and your family ... for my price ..."

"Your price is high!"

"As is the risk," returned the attorney quietly.

"We don't know for certain your scheme will work."

"If it doesn't you will have lost nothing. If it does, Mary of Montlaine will no longer be a problem. With Mary out of the way we shall be able to settle the estate quickly, quietly and in your favor."

"Very well then, I will communicate your plans to my brother Duncan. We shall be in touch."

"Duncan is nearby, then?"

Mr. Echworth looked surprised. "But no, he is, as you know, still in London."

"I see. Then I suppose I shall have to wait ... more than a week's time for my answer?"

"Perhaps, Mr. Parks ... perhaps not. It is a family matter and Duncan is the head of the family. However, we shall see." He got to his feet, donned his hat on his perfectly dressed hair and walked leisurely out of the tavern.

Edward Parks sighed, set himself back on his chair and watched Echworth depart. His large hand rubbed his mouth, which had become dry with their discussion, and then he motioned the barmaid to bring him an ale. The sun was setting outdoors, and Montlaine would soon be riding, making for his cavern hideaway. He thought of his friend and sighed.

Chapter Eight

Richard of Grey shrugged himself out of his super-fine blue coat, undid his cravat, unbuttoned his pale-blue silk waistcoat and proceeded alone down the narrow wooded path that skirted Penrod Park. It had been a miserable morning, a vexing lunch and a boring afternoon. With all this, if it wasn't enough to try any man's soul, his sister had vanished and he didn't know where to begin to look for her.

"Damn!" he said out loud, threw his coat over his shoulder and kicked out at a stone. However, a sound not far ahead brought him up short. "Who's there?" He received no answer, but he definitely heard the thud of a light foot on earth.

"Devil a bit if that is you, Ness! Come on...stop your games!" Still no answer. He threw his coat on the ground in total exasperation, gave out a yell and started in hot pursuit. This was it. He had had enough. He was in this horrible county because of her pranks, started by his cousin, who was now stealing a march on him with the lovely Sheila Echworth. He was going to catch Ness and he was going to give her a good talking-to!

He could just make out a female form skirting through the trees. Small, though ... never mind, it had to be Ness. He took a shortcut, jumping over bushes, darting around pines, and then bracing himself against a tree he caught his breath and waited. In a moment he was upon her and had her caught neatly around the waist. "Now you've done it!" he yelled. "With all your kicking you've torn my shirt!"

The struggling girl stopped at once and stood back, her cheeks aflame, her eyes bright. "Oh, I am so sorry ... but you should not have seized me in that fashion."

Totally taken aback, Richard of Grey opened his light-blue eyes wide and stared. "But ... you are not m'sister!"

The dark-eyed girl put a hand to her mouth and giggled. "Of course not, silly."

He surveyed his prize in stupefaction. Here was a slip of a woman. No more than fifteen to be sure, yet well on her way to womanhood and still a child. A strangely enticing mixture. Dark short curls bounced round an adorably pixielike countenance. "But ... but ... then who are you?"

"You should first be begging my pardon, sir!" said the lady, hands on hips.

"Yes, of course, I do indeed beg your pardon." He then thought better of this. "Hold a moment! What are you doing here at Penrod? You aren't a servant?"

"No, I am not a servant. I am a guest ... but please, sir, it is a secret." Her hand went toward him with her plea, and he found himself patting it assuringly.

"A secret, is it?" He looked round for a place to sit, found a weathered log and drew her to it. "Perhaps then you should tell me who you are and why it is a secret."

She smiled warmly. She knew who he was and trusted him. Instinct ruled, and so she allowed him to draw her out.

She told him all, and when she was done she found a young man outraged and willing to take on her cause. Then it was she asked him why it was he was skulking about in the woods and he told her of his infatuation with Sheila Echworth. Mary's face went sour.

"Sheila? Oh, I must say that is a poor choice indeed!"

He took instant umbrage. She was an appealing child but a child all the same and shouldn't be passing judgments on her elders.

"My dear child, you know nothing of such matters!"

"No, that is true. But I have been giving the matter a great deal of thought, Richard...I may call you that?" She waited for him to nod. "Yes, well, I have been giving the matter my consideration...about boys and girls...courting...and I think 'tis a great deal of nonsense. If a man wants a woman, he should tell her...she should tell him. Why do they play at games, which is what Sheila does? She is playing you off your cousin. I know because I watched from my peephole..."

"You little minx! Your peephole indeed! Where is this peephole?"

"I won't tell you. It isn't my secret to tell. 'Tis Lady Penrod's."

"Damn if I let it go at that! I'm not about to go sporting around a place with people spying on me!"

"I wasn't spying, you silly thing. You and your sister, not to mention your cousin, have made things very uncomfortable for me. It was lonely enough before...but now I am forever in my room, coming out through hidden stairwells...so the other night when you were all in the parlor, I amused myself by sitting at my peep-hole. You wouldn't have minded if I was in the room, would you?"

"No, but . . ."

"No buts. 'Tis the same thing. After all . . . you weren't alone with Sheila . . . so I wasn't spying."

"You have an odd way of putting things, my girl. What if we said something about you . . . not knowing you were listening?"

"You did. Well, not you precisely, but Sheila described me to you and your cousin as a horried, ungrateful viper."

"Did she?" returned Ricky surprised. "I don't remember that."

"You were too busy mooning about over her."

"Never mind!" He looked about and saw the sun was setting. "We had better be getting back, and tonight, my dear, no sneaking about. You'll have dinner with us in style."

Her eyes took on a frightened expression. "I . . . I can't . . ."

He frowned. "No one will hurt you child."

"Your sister . . . your cousin . . . they might let some word slip . . ."

"My sister and cousin are totally trustworthy. They won't give you away. And Mary . . . no one will dare touch you . . . certainly not the Echworths."

"Richard, you don't know . . . you just don't know!"

Lady Vanessa brushed her long auburn waves into a semblance of silk. She looked into her mirror at her creamy complexion but saw instead the day she had passed. Frustrating. To be so close to questioning the Widdons girl and yet unable to get the job done! Maddening. It had been uncomfortable as well. She had found her way easily enough to Widdons's mill and had made up a lame excuse for wanting to see Bess Widdons. They had told her she could wait, but after an hour passed, Mr. Widdons suggested she go up to the house. There she waited another hour and the girl never appeared. Where was she? No one knew and no one seemed to care. Finally she had given it up and left.

Vanessa clasped pearl drops to her ears. She felt restless and listless. She wasn't really concerned with her appearance or with the fact that the gold silk gown became her figure stunningly. Dinner was bound to be dull, what with Rick and Randy all agog over Sheila and talking of nothing else. Again she sighed. She had almost taken the turn for Bodmin Heights...for the ocean...for the viscount's cave. She had stopped herself, though. It was absurd. Why should she go to him? She had nothing to tell him. Whims and impulses, they would see her ruined, she told herself, and thus she steeled herself and came straight to Penrod instead.

It wasn't much later when dinner was over and she found herself once again in the quiet of her room. An odd sort of conversation at dinner. She hadn't felt like talking. Randy talked of nothing but Sheila, which was to be expected, but Rick had been unusually quiet. After dinner he announced that he was going into town. Randy went off to join him, and she was left to Lady Penrod. Augusta had always a way of drawing her out.

"Ness, love...you were gone for most of the day?"

"Yes," said Lady Vanessa cautiously.

"Ah, you don't trust me," said her ladyship on a hurt note.

Ness could not resist her. "Stop it! You play the part badly. You are steaming with curiosity, not concern!"

Augusta Penrod rapped her charge's knuckles with

89

her embroidered fan. "You are very rude to see through me. Now, out with it, what *have* you been doing all day?"

"I went to see the vicar!"

"You never . . . oh, Ness, what am I going to do with you? Well, go on, what came of it?"

"This. It seems the vicar had a *tendre* for Melony Fry, who was, according to Taby, the vicar's housekeeper, a heathen tart. Guss, I must tell you that I don't like Vicar Poole . . . there is something about him that . . . puts me off."

"But you didn't spend the entire day with a man you found you disliked?"

"No, I went on . . . but I shan't tell you about that. Not yet."

"Why not?"

"I have my reasons. Now, you tell me . . . about Mary?"

"What about Mary?"

"When is she going to come out of hiding?"

"Not yet . . . though I admit, it can't go on forever."

"Hmmm. At any rate . . . it is just as well for the time being."

"What have you in mind, Ness?" asked Augusta on a worried note.

"Naught."

They had left it at that, played a round of cards, and then each had retired to their own room. Vanessa strolled out onto her terrace. The moon was half hidden behind masses of clouds. The park below with its neat lawns and orderly flower beds seemed serene. Vanessa ran a hand over her gold silk gown, for she was doing a battle with her will. Calm yourself . . . read a book . . . no! She could stand it no more.

Off went the ribbons holding her in orderly fashion.

Off went the jewels, the gold silk slippers, the elegant gown. Quickly she rummaged through her trunk for the breeches she always kept on hand. She pulled these on, shrugged herself into a white linen shirt and slipped a dark cloak round her shoulders.

Gingerly she opened her door. No one about. Hurriedly she took the stairs to the main hall below. Down the corridor to the ballroom and out the long glass doors to the garden. There she stood and sucked in the cool night air before making for the stables.

The grooms and livery boys were in the loft drinking, eating and joking loudly. She slinked in, took her mare by the halter and moved her out, reaching for the bit and bridle as she passed out the door. Once outside she drew on her mare's bridle, putting the leather halter aside. "Here, mare . . ." She drew her to the fence, which she used to aid her to mount on the horse's bare back. Gathering up her reins, she jogged her horse off down the drive, across the road and toward the open field.

The viscount of Montlaine finished brushing his stallion down, threw some hay into the makeshift stable and turned away. His mood was strange, and he found it difficult being honest with himself. He rolled up his shirtsleeves and moved outdoors. There he climbed upon a favorite incline made up of small boulders of various sizes and crouched to gaze out on the dark modulating brine. Again and against his will her face came to mind. Gray eyes twinkling, pert nose in the air, cherry lips pursed in thought, auburn softness framing her lovely face . . . Naughty Lady Ness. He wondered if she was all they said, and something inside hoped that she was not . . . for they painted a picture of a spoiled girl who broke hearts without a care.

Vanessa dismounted and took her mare carefully

down the sandy path to the narrow beach below. They wound their way past heavy boulders, through the splashing tide coming in, and then a piece of whiteness in the dark sky caught her eye and she stopped.

He was getting up from his crouched position, and she couldn't say a word as she watched him. His silky black hair blew around his lean rugged face. His shirt billowed away from his hard bronzed body, showing to advantage the powerful lines. She discovered in that moment that she was attracted to him, and her lovely arched brow went up. Oh no, she told herself, not this one . . . 'twould be too dangerous to care for a rogue. Thus, satisfied with her self-control, she moved forward.

The viscount of Montlaine saw her all at once. His satanic-shaped brows moved with his surprise. His mind urged caution. Nimbly he jumped down from his heights and waited for her to approach. As she drew near, the candlelight from his open cave flickered brightly over her flowing auburn hair, and he was conscious of a certain fluttering within his veins. She was certainly a desirable woman, and he had not had a woman in some time. Was Naughty Lady Ness after a little excitement? His heart hardened as this thought jumped to the fore.

He gave her a slight bow, and his voice dripped with sarcasm.

"Ah, my lady Vanessa, laden no doubt with supper for a hungry man?"

She heard the tone in his voice, but mistook its meaning. Her finely arched brows drew together and her voice held concern.

"Oh, but you can see I have brought nothing. Goodness, my lord, I didn't realize that I should . . ."

He had taken up her reins and was leading her into his cave, but at this he stopped and laughed. "So, Lady Vanessa does not deign to bother with excuses?"

She watched him tether her horse. "Excuses?" Sudden dawning brought the color to her cheeks. She didn't know which feeling towered, shame or anger. "I...I didn't think I needed an excuse."

He had moved toward her. Imperceptibly his hand had undone the ribbon holding her cloak on her shoulders. He watched it drop to the ground and felt his blood stirred. "No, Lady Vanessa doesn't give a brace of snaps for the proprieties when her desires are at stake! She will don a boy's breeches...take to her horse...bareback in the dead of night in order to visit a demon in his cave dwelling. Why? Because it is exciting, is it not?"

His voice had dropped to a husky caress, and his hands had found their way to her small waist. In an instant he had her drawn into a passionate embrace. His kiss took them both by surprise. Neither thought it possible that they could experience the excitement, the ardor, the dizziness that ran through them, for both thought themselves—for various reasons—quite immune to such things.

Lady Vanessa had not borne three London seasons without having experienced the kisses of sophisticated men. She had never before found that a kiss could do what it did now. Why did she lose all feeling in her knees? Why did everything, the cave, the ceiling, the walls, converge into a sheet of darkness within which fireworks exploded? What was happening? Why did the blood in her veins burn? Hold! Her mind shouted at her to get hold. She managed to put a hand to his iron chest, and this proved to be so thrilling that she immediately dropped her hand and stood back from him, hoping avidly that he could not hear the beating of her pulsating heart.

She managed to form some words, and her tone held no fear.

"Tell me, my lord . . . do you mean to ravish me?" She indicated only casual interest.

The viscount of Montlaine wanted this woman with her tantalizing body and her sweet lips, but he heard this and let go a gusty laugh. She was a handful, this chit. Intriguing in every quarter, inciting more, much more, than passion. "No, acquit me of that, my beauty." He let go a sigh and his finger stroked her cheek. "Though if you wish me to seduce you, it would be my pleasure."

She made an excellent show of disappointment. "Oh dear, now you've made a muddle of it, haven't you? I mean, really, my lord, the very least you could do is to make a push at getting me into that straw bed of yours. After all, it is a well-known fact that we daughters of earls do enjoy an exciting toss in the hay now and then!" At which she nearly stomped her foot.

He could see her gray eyes blazing with anger. She was certainly outspoken. Why didn't she slap his face, stomp off in outrage? What sort of woman came out to a strange man like this, allowed him to kiss her—for allow him she had—and then put him in his place soundly for doing it?

He grinned in spite of her restrained fury. "Shall I answer you in the manner you deserve? Yes, I think so, Naughty Lady Ness." His grinned widened at her expression. "Yes, your reputation has followed you to Cornwall, and then what do I find but the Naughty Lady in my cave . . . without evident reason. I kissed the Naughty Lady and she allowed it, but ah, she would have it said the demon ravished her ... not seduced her."

She felt her anger well up, and then she saw the humor of it and laughed. "You are certainly a fiend to throw my reputation into my face! Especially in light of yours."

He was pouring out a glass of white wine, putting it in her hands. "So then our reputations make us friends? So be it, we shall call a truce."

She sipped the wine and wrinkled her nose. "A reputation is an odd thing, is it not? There has always got to be a reason for it all, and the reason is nearly always idiotic."

"Perhaps ... though *I* certainly gave the gossip mongers cause for their prattle."

"Your London excursion into vice. I have been wondering about it. Whatever could have moved you to take such a course? After all my lord, you weren't in the first blush, were you? I mean, I should think you had gone that route during your salad days!"

He turned and gave her his chin. "I wouldn't call seven and twenty being in my dotage, sweetheart!"

"No, nor would I ... but then, as I said, there is always a reason, and yours couldn't have been sowing wild oats."

"No, you think not? I came home from the war, perhaps a bit disillusioned ... tired, wanting a little freedom ..."

"That doesn't fadge. You are giving me a round tale, and it won't do. I would rather you didn't say anything if you are going to tell me a lie." She frowned at his silence. "You mustn't be fearful of shocking me. You know I have a brother, and we are in the habit of exchanging the most outrageous confidences, so I am not easily put off."

He put up his hand. "Do you know, I am inclined to believe what they say about you!"

"Are you? You will be sadly out, then, for my life is tragically dull compared to what they say. But let us not change the subject."

"The subject, eh? Am I to take it that my life is the subject at hand?"

She smiled benignly. "Dearest demon, you know that it is, and I shan't tell you why I am here until you confess all. It was a woman . . . wasn't it?"

He looked at her sharply. "You are very perceptive."

She inclined her head and sighed. "I should love for you to go on thinking so, but I am not really. *You,* my lord, are a romantic. You would like to appear a cynic, but you see I am well acquainted with a real cynic, and you are nothing to Byron. So, shall I guess what she did, or will you tell me?"

He gave up. She seemed to draw on his very soul, this bright beauty with her inquiring gray eyes. "As you say . . . I am, or rather *was,* something of a romantic. When I saw her for the first time I was four and twenty and thought she was an angel."

"No woman is an angel," put in Ness.

"So I came to realize. She was not much younger than I and I was off to war. She promised to wait. I had reason to think she would."

"I am surprised she did not!" exclaimed Vanessa at once. "You are out of the ordinary good-looking, virile, titled, wealthy . . . good lord, the girl must have . . ."

"Aimed her sights higher!" He put in on a note of contempt. "Though I thank you for your flattery."

"'Twasn't flattery, my lord. Well then, she did not wait?"

"No, she took on a lover . . . some brawny servant, I was told."

"But you said she went for higher stakes?"

"*If* you will allow me to continue?" he shot back at her. "Well now, how does the story go? Ah, the angel of my dreams got herself with child and therefore could not wait for me. No, she found herself an ancient duke, and within a short span of time managed to convince him the child was his." He looked away a moment and said lightly, "From all accounts they seem reasonably content with one another. So then, a sad story ends well."

Lady Vanessa plumped herself down on a pile of clean straw and took a longer gulp of wine. His story provoked many contrary feelings. At last she looked up at his face and pulled a grimace. "Oh, don't look such an injured puppy! What an innocent you were to care for someone of her character, and how very, very naive you were at four and twenty! Faith, I am but one and twenty and have a great deal more sense than you did then. Tell me, for a creature of her stamp...you plunged yourself into hell?"

He had never been dressed down by a woman, especially a woman upon whom, for some inexplicable logic, he wished to make a favorable impression. He was taken aback and stumbled to his defense.

"You don't understand...I thought her..."

"I know, indeed you have said, you thought her an angel! That, my poor demon, does not excuse you."

"Excuse...*me?*" He was greatly astounded by her reasoning.

"Well, really, how dare you think...expect anyone to be perfect? You saw a beautiful woman and immediately expected her to conform to your notions of what she should be. You created a personality around her, never bothering to look within the girl, never bothering with the workings of her mind."

He put up his hands. "Enough! If you are trying to say I wronged the lady...so be it, I am paying for it now."

"You wronged yourself!" She sighed. "But that has naught to do with now. Now is something else. Oh dear...but never mind, we shall get through it."

"Shall *we*? Pray...how will *we* accomplish such a feat? The odds, you know, are not in our favor."

"Odds? What do I care for odds? I am not a gambler, my lord. I believe in working with what I can see." She downed the remainder of her wine and went back on her elbows. There was a light in her gray eyes that bewitched him. He found himself gazing into her face, almost losing himself, his troubles in the softness of her smile. She brought him back to reality.

"My lord...things are black...I shan't try to do you up brown with a round tale or two...but this afternoon I discovered something I think might be helpful to you in the future."

"So then the Naughty Lady did have a reason for entering the demon's den!"

She giggled. "Alas, the truth destroys my heady reputation. Indeed, I did not come here to be ravished."

He dropped down to the straw beside her, and she gave him an arched look. "*My lord*...every propriety is offended!"

"But are you?"

"No, not in the least." There was a softness in her voice, but because his black eyes drew her to him she looked away a moment and composed herself. "So then, I am here to tell you that I paid a visit today to Vicar Poole. Sad to say, my lord, the good vicar did not hold you in great esteem!"

The viscount smiled ruefully. "That is putting it gently. The vicar despised me."

"Why?"

"I offended *his* sense of propriety." The viscount gave a short laugh.

"Yes, but more than that, you, my lord, had the audacity to dally with Melony Fry publicly, and I believe the good vicar wanted the girl for himself!"

"Did he?" The viscount sat back to gaze at her in some amazement. "Will you never cease to surprise me, sweetheart?"

"There, you have said it again. I let it pass the first time, for I suppose it is part of your cavalier fashion, but I am afraid it rankles. I am *not* your sweetheart. We called a truce, and declared ourselves friends." She waited for him to concede this point. He inclined his head and restrained his quivering lip. She took a breath of air and continued, "Very well, then, back to the vicar. His testimony, you see, would be quite prejudiced. That is a fact we could use in court to our favor... that is, assuming that we have to go to court to clear your name." She put up her hand to stop him from interrupting. "Secondly, I discovered from the vicar's housekeeper that Melony had but one friend... a Bess Widdons, do you know her?"

He frowned and shook his head. "No, how should I? I scarcely knew Melony. She was a pretty lass... I passed a few moments with her now and then... nothing more." He shook his head. "Where does this lead?"

"I am not precisely sure. I tried to speak to Bess Widdons today, but she was not to be found. An odd thing... her family didn't seem interested in her whereabouts or her doings." She shrugged. "Never mind, I shall try again on the morrow."

She pushed herself upward with her hands, but his grip held her wrist, turned her in the straw to face him, and his eyes stayed her in a way peculiar to himself.

"Why, Vanessa?"

"Why what, my lord?"

"Why are you going to so much trouble over me?"

"Over you? I don't know that I am going to any trouble over you precisely. You have a sister . . . and if I believe that you have been used in this plot as you say you have, then I am afraid your sister is in danger."

"Then your efforts are for Mary?" He waited quietly for his answer.

Vanessa had waltzed her way through three London seasons. She was hailed the incomparable. She was toasted a charmer, a wit, a very naughty but thoroughly enchanting lady, and still she had conducted herself throughout with honesty. She didn't like to play games. Yet her ever-present candor could not be called upon in this instance. She couldn't blurt out that she hadn't even met his young sister yet. She didn't know why, she only knew she could not admit to this. "Let us say that Naughty Lady Ness is once again after a little excitement. What else have I to do in Cornwall?"

He allowed her to get to her feet. He followed suit. He was dissatisfied with her response. A little angry too, though he knew not why. He retrieved her cloak, slipped it around her shoulders, stood back as she released her horse. They laughed as the stallion whinnied sharply to see the pretty mare leave, and then he was walking with her down the narrow stretch of sand to the winding incline that would take her over the moors and back to Penrod.

She tilted her head and gave him a warm smile. "May I beg a leg up, my lord?" She could have used a rock to help her mount her unsaddled horse, but she was not averse to a mild flirtation.

He teased, "Cannot the indomitable lady find a way to scramble up her mare's back?"

100

"I don't think that is worthy of you, my lord. Indeed, this carefree life has stolen your manners." She gave him a mock sigh. "If I have to . . . I could, you know. Make no mistake."

He laughed. "I don't doubt it, my lady." He put his hands beneath her bent knee and said softly, "On the count of three, love?"

The numbers counted, he hoisted her so that she landed neatly and gently on her mare's back. His hand rested a moment on her thigh. "You will take care riding over the moors?"

"I will, make yourself easy." She started her horse off and then stopped to look around. "You will miss me terribly if I don't come tomorrow night, you know."

"And why wouldn't you come?" His grin was wide, and he felt ridiculously young.

"Because you haven't asked me to, my lord." She was twinkling, lingering in the shadow, exciting his heart.

"I hadn't asked you to come this night, my lady . . . but you came all the same!" he pointed out blandly.

She chuckled. "You are, of course, being quite horrid! Well then, I shall leave you to wonder about tomorrow night!" With a slight pressure of her leg, she moved her mare forward and it was not long before she was out of sight.

Chapter Nine

Lord Richard of Grey descended the main staircase. His gaze seemed fixed upon the oriental rug trailing beneath his lackadaisical descent. However, had his sister been priviliged to observe, she would have raised a brow. Richard of Grey was troubled!

The hour was early, the light dim and the day promising rain. His sparkling cravat had not been given the usual attention and hung in a manner that would have pained Brummell. His delicately embroidered pale-blue waistcoat was still unbuttoned beneath his dark-blue superfine. He stopped at the foot of the stairs and put a finger to his thin pursed bottom lip, but his thoughts were soon interrupted by the ever attentive Toby, who appeared from the dark hallway.

"Oh . . . good morning, sir."

"What? Oh, yes . . . good morning to you, Toby."

"Cook has just got the fire lit in the kitchen, sir, and your coffee won't be but a moment. If I may suggest, sir, a nice fire is working in the library. I shall be happy to bring your coffee to you there."

"The library?" returned Richard absently. "Yes . . . the library." With which he crossed the polished oak floor to a pair of double doors which Toby hastened to open.

Once within and alone, Richard reflected on the things that were troubling him, his sister's doings taking top priority among these. She was his magical being, his cherished friend. He had adored her all the years he was growing, and though the world might dub her naughty, he knew there were few better than Vanessa. Rarely did he criticize, or even interfere in her antics. She always came about. But this time . . . this time perhaps it was time he stepped in? How to do such a thing? He was her junior. He was her pet. How could he make himself her guardian in this instance? A problem indeed, and one that had to be attended to immediately, for this time she would not confide in him. He shook his head and moved to the fireplace mantel shelf, where his elbow found a resting place and his fist pressed his mouth. Last evening's episode was still very vivid in his mind.

He had returned early from town, leaving his cousin to while away the midnight hour there. The stables were dark, but even so one of the grooms had called from his room above that he would be right down. He had told the lad there was no need and proceeded to untack his horse. This done, the tack put away, he moved to snuff the wall candle when he noticed Shadow's empty stall.

He went outside and waited, and it wasn't long before he saw the gleam of the mare's bright coat. He stepped around the stable to await Vanessa in quiet. He watched as she dismounted outside the building, untacked her horse, unbridled the mare and put her away.

She hung up her tack and stepped gingerly without

and would have then proceeded to slink back to the house had he not touched her arm. She nearly shrieked but stopped herself in time as she spun around to discover her brother.

"Zounds . . . Rick, you startled me!"

"Did I?" His face and tone were drawn in quiet disapproval.

Few could deter Vanessa from an object once she had it in sight. Few could persuade her she was wrong when she was certain she was in the right of it. However, Richard in his gentleness had always that power. "Ah, you are put out with me? Really, Rick, there is no need to fret. No one saw me go out . . . no one shall see me go in."

"That is not the point, though."

"Is it not?" She was teasing.

"This is serious, Ness . . . I am serious." His eyes were dark with his gravity.

"Yes, I can see that you are, but you needn't be, Rick. I can take care of myself . . . I shan't do anything wrong."

"But you already have. You just can't go jauntering about the countryside in the dark, by yourself, dressed as you are. Ness . . . people would be bound to think the most ugly things . . ."

"Would they? Did you think an ugly thought, Rick, when you saw me ride up tonight?" Her brows were drawn tightly, and there was a catch in her voice.

He shook his head. "Don't be stupid! *I know you!*"

"Even so, you would like to know what I was about?" She was looking intently into his eyes.

He frowned. "I really didn't think about *that* . . . I supposed you were restless and out for a bit of air. But Ness . . . are you up to something?"

"If I told you, love, you would only fret, so I shan't

105

tell you yet, but if you are so worried about what people might think you will lend me your aid and make sure they don't find out!" Again she was teasing, trying to bring him back into spirits.

He opened his eyes wide and nearly took a step backward. "Never say you mean to continue to...oh, Ness...do say you are only bamming me!"

She reached out and touched his cheek. "No one will know who I am dressed in this manner."

"But the stableboys?"

"They did not see."

"What if they came down and noticed Shadow missing?"

"Yes, I see I shall have to think of something to tell them in advance so that this won't cause a bother," she said thoughtfully.

"But...but Ness...why? What are you up to? What is towards?"

"Never mind, Rick, and don't look so worried! I shan't go gallivanting every night. I do promise *that!*"

He shook his head and walked her to the house and the rear entrance. There he told her to wait until he entered from the front and made certain all was clear. This he had done. But now in the light of day he was fairly convinced that he would have to do something to curtail her effectively. But what?

A lackey appeared with the coffee, set it in place and quietly vanished. Richard sighed and poured himself a cup, dropped a quantity of cream into the steaming blackness and took a sip.

"Pssst!"

With eyes open wide, Richard scanned the room, looking for the cause of the almost-human sound. Finding himself alone, he shrugged and again put the cup of coffee to his lips.

106

"Pssst! I say...Richard, over here!" came the low whisper.

He spun around and stared at the wainscoting. There, to his amazement, a section of the heavy paneling was opened into the room. In its undersized portal stood a dark-haired, dark-eyed minx of a girl in a white ankle-length schooldress. She was waving him forward anxiously.

"Mary!" he said out loud.

She immediately put her finger to her mouth and pulled a face. "Do come...and hurry...oh, and bring some of those biscuits, for I have finished mine and I am still famished!"

Excited about the prospect of exploring secret staircases, he took no time out to examine the wisdom of this plan. He quickly filled a linen napkin with the buns and biscuits on his tray and hurried to bend his head and enter the nether realms of Penrod Tower.

"By Jupiter, this is famous!" exclaimed Richard once she had closed the secret door and stood to face him.

"Yes, it is rather nice...though at Montlaine we have many more. We even have a secret room...and a tunnel that leads to the moors!"

"Have you? I daresay your parents closed off the tunnel, though? Dangerous things...never know when one will cave in on you. We had a Jacobean tunnel up at our estate in the north, but m'parents walled it off."

"Well, ours isn't walled off. Though no one uses it, and I don't even know how to get to it. Bret knew, of course..." She turned away.

He put his hand on her shoulder. "Come on, then... show me where this leads...and here, take one of these to munch on."

She beamed up at him and obediently began devouring the bun he had shoved into her hand. Up the

107

narrow winding stone steps, one, two, three flights until they reached a dark wood panel. A spring released this, and they were pushing it open into a bright and amazingly attractive turret room. Circular and with walls of stone, it had a large window on both sides of its large fireplace. Another door led onto a small rectangular battlement, where Mary had chosen to grow herbs and bright flowers to help occupy her time.

She spun around in some excitment and laughed.

"Well . . . is not my prison cozy?"

He had been pleasantly surprised and was about to say this when his eyes lit on the large four-poster bed at his back. He walked away from this to the settee near the window.

"It is very nice, Mary . . . but . . . I shouldn't be here alone with you."

"No, you shouldn't . . . so do step outside with me." She had all the ease of a child, and he smiled as she took his hand and led him out the glass door to the battlement.

The view was breathtaking, and he remarked upon it at once. Mary lowered her eyes and agreed gently. "Yes . . . I can see quite a bit from here." She hesitated a moment, and then, "Where did you and your cousin go last night? To visit Sheila?"

"No . . . though we are having dinner there tonight."

"Are you? Is Lady Penrod going there as well?"

"No . . . she is promised elsewhere . . . but I think that my sister Vanessa joins our party."

"*I* don't think Vanessa likes my cousin Sheila."

"Now how would you know? Spying from your peephole again, Mary?"

She stomped her foot. "If you are going to be horrid . . . you may leave!"

"Why didn't you join us for dinner last night?" he

asked, ignoring her scolding.

She sighed, "I wanted to...but, oh, Richard...it just wouldn't be wise. If the Echworths know I am here, they will make me return to Montlaine with them...and I would rather live in exile than do that!"

"But Mary..."

"Anyway, what difference does it make to you? You want me to return to Montlaine because it is what they want! And of course, you want...whatever Sheila wants!" She was out of temper with him.

"That is a silly thing to say," he returned.

"Is it? Then why do you want me to show myself?"

"Because I know you cannot run away from your problems, you have to face up to them!"

"I am not running away from a problem, Richard! I am running away from a *murderer!*"

"What?"

"Richard, really...why else do you think Lady Penrod feels it necessary to seclude me?"

"I...I..."

"You didn't think, did you?"

"No, I suppose not."

"My brother was innocent. Obviously then someone else is guilty. Who then? It is very simple when you think about it. Who would stand to gain? The Echworths. So what have we? A plan to discredit my brother...perhaps get him hanged. Instead, fate played in their favor...the war did not kill him...but the villagers..." She was pacing. "Duncan Echworth will now gain the title and half the wealth. The other half goes to me. They have two alternatives. I can be eliminated...or married to Duncan."

"You are too young to be married!" returned Richard vehemently.

She put up her chin. "Well...perhaps...but other

109

girls have been married at fifteen. It doesn't signify, for Duncan despises me. I used to kick him in the shins when I was younger."

"Then I don't blame the fellow," said Richard.

She stuck out her tongue in an unladylike gesture and proceeded casually, "What then must they do to get their grip around the entire Montlaine fortune?"

"Must they have the entire fortune? Perhaps they are not greedy?"

"Richard ... you are most naive! If they went to the trouble of eliminating my brother ... destroying his reputation ... they are then quite, quite greedy, for you must know that my brother has always seen them out of debt. Bret was always very generous to them ..." her voice trailed off.

He put a comforting arm around her shoulder. "There, there ... this is all speculation ..."

"But who else could have done it?"

"There is always the possibility that ... that you were wrong about your brother ..."

She stepped back as though he had struck her. "Get out!"

"Mary ..."

"I was wrong about you, I want you to leave now."

"Mary ... look, I am sorry."

"As you should be, but that does not change your mind, does it? No, I quite see you are only sorry that you have hurt me. You would rather believe in the Echworths ... because of Sheila ... than believe in Bret ... because of me!"

"And if I believed in your brother's innocence ... because of you, solely on your word ... then the people I am dining with tonight are possibly the wickedest lot I have ever come across. Just think about that before you flare up at me for my doubts!" With which he turned on his heel.

She ran after him. "Richard!"

He turned, but she found she could not say the words that came to mind. Instead, "You may use the regular door and take the main staircase ... no one will notice at this hour." She watched him go in silence. There was one thing he was right about, she couldn't go on like this indefinitely!

Vanessa heard her maid draw back her curtains. She picked up her head from the pillow she had been nuzzling, opened one eye, groaned and dropped back upon her pillow.

"I've left ye yer coffee, m'lady ... and there be freshly baked scones and biscuits as well ..."

"Thank you, Millie ..." came the muffled response.

The elderly woman was not offended. She had been caring after Lady Vanessa's person too long to take umbrage over her vagaries. She had been wanting a nice chat with her young mistress, but she could see Lady Vanessa would not be talkative this morning. Nevertheless she made an attempt.

"Coo, but the weather be fair to keeping us indoors today ..."

"What?" Lady Vanessa jumped up to a sitting position and rubbed her eyes hard, shaking off the last dreamy remnants of her sleep. It was then that she heard it at her window. The unmistakable static of rain cutting through the air. She gazed out her window at the dark sky, the black swiftly moving clouds, followed by greater masses. "Oh, no ..." she wailed.

"What then? Did ye 'ave somethin' special planned, love?" sympathized her maid with a shake of her mop-capped head.

"Something special? No ... but I did want to visit with someone ..."

"Well then ... can ye not go in the coach?" was the

111

surprised return. Millie never understood why her mistress always preferred to ride a horse. Horses were to her miserable beasts, ungrateful and untrustworthy. One might be feeding them a carrot one moment and getting nipped the next.

Lady Vanessa quickly thought this over. It would look odd if she were to arrive in state at the Widdons's home. It might arouse suspicion. The Echworths might hear of it . . . wonder about it. No. She would not be calling on Bess Widdons today. Drat!

"Thank you, Millie," she said quietly.

The elderly woman knew well her mistress wanted to be alone. With a sigh she shuffled toward the door. "Ye'll find I've laid out yer pretty pink muslin, m'lady . . . ye'll ring when ye want me?"

"That I will, Millie." And again she looked out the window. As her bedroom door closed and left her alone she sat back heavily and released only a small fraction of her frustration—"Fiend seize this weather!"

Chapter Ten

Leaves of brass wound their way ornately among pear-shaped crystal droplets. The candles set in wild profusion between these gave off an almost mystical haze. A fire crackled in the large stone hearth. Conversation seemed to flow easily, almost musically, among the gathered assembly in the Montlaine library. Dinner had been on the whole a successful affair, and the Echworths were disposed to being amiable.

A glass of Madeira had been placed in Lady Vanessa's hand. She smiled sweetly at Orson Echworth, thanked him and moved away toward the chamber's dominating feature, its full-length portrait of the viscount astride Midnight. Silently, slightly, only very slightly did she lift her glass to the painting and take a sip. A mistake perhaps.

"No doubt you feel he was worthy of your toast," said Orson at her back.

She did not acknowledge this by turning his way. She answered him, though, with a question: "Do you not?"

He shrugged his shoulders. "He was certainly a good

soldier, I am told...had quite a command under him...but the recent past explains that."

"Does it?"

"Why, yes. My cousin was ever after excitement. The war gave him that. Once home he had to find a new means to fill his needs."

She stared up at his face now. The firelight glinted in his gray eyes. She wanted to slap him. Instead, she did something better. She turned her attention once more to the painting.

"And even knowing that, you are still fascinated with his portrait."

"Does that so bother you?"

"Very much. He seems even in death to capture the interest of a beautiful woman...the only woman I would have look my way."

"You are very bold," said Vanessa, a curve to her cherry lips.

"As bold as *his* portrait?"

She laughed. "You would not be comfortable in such a stance. Admit it, sir!"

He nodded. "In truth, I would not, but if that is what it would take to fix your interest..."

She moved away, and her gaze this time came to rest on a large sandy-haired gentleman, Mr. Edward Parks. He was an interesting figure, his status an odd one. By his own admission he was the late viscount's close confidant and solicitor, yet here he was giving every indication that he was very much enamored of Miss Echworth.

"Your sister is looking well," said Vanessa, changing the subject, and indeed Sheila, gowned in gold, her ginger locks curled effectively around her pretty face, was looking exceptional this evening.

"Sheila...hmmm...and why not, with three eligible bachelors to preen for?" He took up Vanessa's hand. "But you are changing the subject." His lips brushed her fingertips ever so lightly, and he found the sensation thrilling. Her eyes, gray like his own, but full with sparkle, emotion. He knew in that instant that he wanted her.

She felt something of this and pulled away gently. "And what was the subject, sir? Some nonsense about changing . . . for a woman?" She shook a finger at him. "You should never alter your ways to please some fickle female . . . unless the change pleases you as well."

"Then you will be delighted to know that I have never attempted to alter my character for a woman. In fact, my pretty, you may find this difficult to believe, but I am not generally in the petticoat line!"

"Are you not?" She shook her head. "Indeed, you are right there, for I do find that hard to believe." She studied him pointedly. "I see you as a heartbreaker."

He stiffened. "Do you? No, I leave that to Duncan, my brother. Alas, sad to say the women are only interested in my taste for clothing, my knack with flower arranging, my superior knowledge of decorating. It has been said that I care more for the cut of my coat than the cut of . . . er . . . a lady's leg."

"Well, I must say that you have succeeded in surprising me. With your dark-gray eyes, your very bright yellow curls, your rogue smile, I put you as a devil with the ladies."

He inclined his head. "Shall I thank you? Would you prefer it if I were a rake? Would that make me more desirable to you? It has been my experience that women are forever allowing themselves to be taken in by such scamps."

"They are a challenge to our powers, you see." She laughed easily.

115

"But you have not answered my question, pretty Lady Vanessa."

"Which is?"

"Would I be a target for your arrow if I were more like my brother Duncan?"

"And Duncan is the rogue . . . the rake . . . the charmer?"

"He is!"

"How shall I answer that? I shall just have to wait for his arrival before I give you my answer." She hesitated. "But tell me . . . as your older brother, does he lord it over you?"

"No. Duncan and I are closer than you can imagine. Whatever has been mine in my youth I have gladly shared with him."

"And of course he will share all that is his with you? Even his inheritance?" she put in archly.

He inclined his head. "I trust that he will. I have no need to concern myself about that."

"Yet, he will get the title," she baited him. There had to be some envy. It just wasn't natural for there to be not one infinitesimal grain of envy between brothers so near to an immense inheritance. She was looking for the weak joint.

Again that enigmatic smile. "Duncan will make better use of it, as he has the gift of leadership I never have known. There too, as I have said, Duncan is the ladies' man, and the ladies do love a title!"

Vanessa could find nothing in the eyes, in the tone, in the facial expression to belie his words. Evidently Orson was not jealous of his brother. Very well, then, all the more reason for aiding his brother to inherit . . . but Duncan had been in London during the time of all the trouble. Surely Orson would not have taken on the scheming alone? No, Orson was not the sort for that.

She could not give up. Somewhere in all this was the answer. She would just have to keep digging. "Of course, there is still the question of your cousin Mary."

"Ah, Mary," he agreed on a sigh.

"A question that has been plaguing us all," put in Edward Parks, suddenly joining their tête-à-tête. His blue eyes studied Vanessa's face intently. She had been an interesting object of scrutiny all evening. Here was the Naughty Lady Ness evidently keeping Montlaine's secret intact. What was her purpose? Was she out for a lark? *Could she be used to advantage?*

Vanessa's sharp gray eyes returned his appraisal. Here was a man who by his own admission was friend to the viscount, yet here he was doing the Echworths up brown. Disgusting! Even so, she found herself liking the man. There was a sincerity to the quick, easy smile. There was a gentleness to his manner.

"I should think as the late viscount's solicitor, you would know where the child might have gone," put in Vanessa, again baiting.

He looked at her sharply. If she could shield Montlaine, why then not Mary? "Alas, all discreet inquiries have turned up naught. Perhaps *you* could hazard a guess, my lady?"

She put a hand to her chest and showed him total astonishment.

"I? But sir, I did not even know the child."

"True, but you passed similar childhoods, I should imagine. Mary was doted upon first by her parents and after their passing by her brother. She was willful... adventurous... and as rumor has it, if you will excuse me, much as you are."

She gave him an arch look. "Do you always put so much credence to rumors? You don't know that I am adventurous, sir."

He grinned. "I beg your pardon if I have offended my lady."

She laughed lightly. "Don't be foolish. I merely point out that it isn't fair to judge someone you have only just met on the gossip you have heard. However, I must admit to a certain willfulness in my character . . . and yes, I enjoy a lark much more than I am told is seemly. Still, I could not hazard a guess to where the child might have gone. You see, I have never had to flee for my life."

This last was gently said, but it left the impact she had intended. Edward Parks stood back to consider this female in a new light. Orson observed Parks's admiring glance and frowned. He drew the lady's attention to himself.

"Granted, then! Let us suppose Mary was so frightened by the villagers, and then later so downcast by her brother's demise, that she sought refuge with someone. I think it is high time that that someone notified us, don't you?"

"An interesting point," returned Parks. "Unless of course, she has gone out of the county and is using some pretext to keep her benefactors from writing to you."

Sheila moved in her chair and made an impatient gesture. "Nonsense, Edward! We all know that Mary can only have gone to Penrod!"

Richard's brows drew together. "But Lady Penrod has told you emphatically that Mary is *not* at Penrod."

Sheila rounded on him and got to her feet. Her gold silk rustled about her slim figure. She was perfectly aware that she had the male attention, and she used it to play off one admirer against the other. "I am surprised at you, Richard. The hour was late the night Mary left Montlaine. There is only one place Mary could have traveled to in the dark of night. She went

118

to Penrod, make no mistake and there she probably still is." She moved to smile at Randy, who made little of all this but was pleased to find her attention upon himself. He returned a devoted smile.

"But Miss Echworth, Lady Penrod has assured you that Mary is *not* within her ken," put in Vanessa sweetly.

"Sooner or later her ladyship will confess the whole."

"You must be very concerned," started Richard.

"Concerned?" let go Sheila unwisely. "We can't move on the inheritance until that dratted child returns to Montlaine!"

"Inheritance? I should think your first concern would be your cousin's safety and welfare," Richard chastised gently.

At last, thought Vanessa with some satisfaction. At last her brother had been shocked by his pretty charmer. She sipped at her light wine and awaited the outcome of all this. Orson moved toward his sister, his countenance exhibiting his checked temper, but it was obvious to Ness that he meant to divert Sheila's remarks. Too late. She was incensed by Richard's gentle admonition. Sheila stamped a gold-slipper-clad foot.

"Richard! You put me all out of patience. Of course our first interest is for my cousin's well-being, which can best be attended to once she is returned to us. A thing I should think you and Randall could help with ... if you would!"

"Help? How?" this from Richard, though Randall too moved forward, his look exhibiting his discomfort and confusion.

"By persuading Lady Penrod to tell us where she has Mary hidden."

"That is enough, Sheila!" snapped Orson, taking over.

She found her brother's eye and her face went white.

Mrs. Echworth assuaged the situation and the uncomfortable silence that followed by taking her daughter's hand and easing her back to her chair. "Yes, really, dear . . ." She turned to the young men. "Do you know that Orson was telling me that there is a boxing match due in Wadbridge village next week?"

Lady Vanessa smiled to see Sheila thus extricated from the awkward subject. No, Mrs. Echworth was no fool. The sort of thing Sheila had been spouting could lead to serious consequences, for the girl had actually accused Lady Penrod of prevarication. Lady Penrod was a powerful woman, too powerful to antagonize, and Mrs. Echworth knew when they were on shaky ground.

Vanessa watched her brother thoughtfully. Odd. He had seemed unusually defensive on the subject of Mary, a girl he knew little or nothing about. Why had he flown into the touchy subject? Why had he taken up a position against his adored Sheila? Well, this was something at least! Perhaps Richard's eyes were opening—not quite all the way, for from the flow of the conversation now, she could see he had already excused his fair charmer (but not perhaps in his mind). Well then, the evening had not been a total waste. She sighed, for she would have to forgo her visit to her devil's den. She had not the excuse of progress to report to him, and to arrive there past midnight without the obvious cause would surely invite his play. That was not something she wanted . . . was it? She turned to his portrait, and Naughty Lady Ness released another sigh.

Lady Vanessa would have been surprised to learn how very near the demon of Montlaine was to her at that very moment. The evening had dragged fretfully by for the viscount. He had not been able to while away

120

the time with reading or with the sketching he so enjoyed. His nerves were alive with anticipation and then later with frustration. He had been looking forward to receiving a visit from Lady Vanessa. Why? He told himself because she had given him hope. He told himself because she was entertaining company, because he was bored, because...because he only wanted her there.

He checked his timepiece and discovered the hour was close onto midnight, and he had an appointment with his man Epps in the Montlaine tunnel.

It was always tricky going from his cave dwelling to the underground tunnel that led to his home. He would as usual have to leave his steed behind and take the moors on foot. His cloak he pulled well over his face and his saturnine eyebrows as he took the lonely stretch of rolling roughland. Aside from low heather and thistle there were no bushes to conceal his movements, and trees were gnarled and scattered. He hugged the high coastline, which was inaccessible from his own beach and cave because of the great jutting divide that stretched into the ocean.

Quickly he scrambled down a rocky hill, leaving Montlaine Castle well in view over his right shoulder, and farther down the high grassy slope to the pebbly beach he had often explored as a boy. Here he moved swiftly, bringing Montlaine closer and still closer into view. He stopped beside a large damp boulder, which he then attacked with a quantity of force until it rolled to reveal a dark gaping hole. He moved within and felt around on the sandy floor for the candle and tinderbox he knew were there. A moment later a lit candle was fixed in its holder. He set it aside on the sandy ground and with the aid of a ring and chain rusty from damp air but deeply embedded in the boulder he pulled the large stone back into its resting place.

Within the air was stale and pungent due to the length of the tunnel, and the viscount wrinkled his nose as he made his way. The narrow corridor rose steadily in its ascent beneath its meadow down. The walls were paved, and heavy oak rafters supported the low ceiling. At its end were stone steps, and these took him to a dark oak panel.

Cautiously he put his ear to the crack between wood and stone wall and listened a moment. Satisfied, he pressed at the hinge which released the panel lock and allowed the door to swing open. He stepped into a pantry closet, blew out his candle and once again put his ear to a door. After a moment he swung the pantry door open into the Montlaine cellar and discovered Epps sitting upon a carton.

The wiry man jumped to his feet and made his master a quick bow. "Lord love ye, but ye be a sight for a worried man."

The viscount grinned. "Worried? About me? What ... did you think the villagers had got me at last?"

"Dinna ye laugh now, m'lord. Strange doing hae been afoot, whot wit them aboovestairs giving a dinner and ye not in yer grave more'n a month!"

The viscount grinned wider. "Shameless crew they are, but who are they entertaining?"

"'Tis Lady Penrod's set that be 'ere ... and what bobbery Mr. Orson and Miss Sheila be up to I can't tell ye ... but word from the kitchen is that both Echworths have an eye to the house of Grey!"

The smile on Montlaine's face vanished. "Lady Vanessa is here, at Montlaine?"

"Lady Vanessa? Aye ... and Orson fair to drooling over her, so they tell me."

"Orson, you say?" The viscount was frowning. "So,

122

she has Orson under her spell? He doesn't usually cavil to the ladies."

"No, nor will the dandy stand a chance wit' sech as her once Duncan arrives."

"And is Duncan arriving?"

"Aye, they expect him inside a week's time."

The viscount picked up his satchel of supplies and moved once again to the pantry closet. Once within, Epps held open the shelved panel that had automatically closed earlier, and the viscount stepped into the tunnel. He turned momentarily. "Epps...keep your ears open for me."

"Aye...but they be tight-lipped around me."

A moment later the lord of Montlaine was gone. Epps turned and his heart nearly dropped to his belly, for there stood Orson Echworth!

Chapter Eleven

Lady Vanessa dismissed her maid and finished changing into her nightdress alone. There was much that was troubling her, and on an impulse she pulled on her ivory silk night wrapper and went to her door, across the polished oak floor and down the corridor to her brother's door. She rapped at it lightly and called his name.

Within his bedchamber Rick stood, still in his shirtsleeves, breeches and boots, contemplating the night from his open window. He heard his sister call and sighed.

"Come in, Ness."

She walked in purposefully, saying his name as she crossed the dark-blue rug. She could see something of his mood already. He was unhappy, reflective, confused. All this she felt, and it showed in his blue eyes as he turned to greet her.

"What brings you at this hour?" He attempted a smile. "I should think you would be abed, dreaming of Orson."

This diverted her purpose momentarily. "Orson?" She gave a short laugh. "Brothers! They know nothing of such things. Did you really think me attracted to Orson?"

"I don't know... you seemed rather interested in him."

"I am interested in him... but not in that way. Now, never mind Orson, I want to talk about you."

"About me?" He eyed his sister warily.

"Yes. I can see you are wrestling with a problem, Rick. You were never able to hide such things from me." She took a step to his bed and plopped herself down comfortably, getting ready for a long chat.

He sighed heavily. Actually, he wanted nothing better than to thrash his thoughts about with his sister. She was always so collected, so calm, so quick to understand. "I can't talk about it. Ness, I made something of a promise... intimated that I would keep mum..."

Vanessa was perceptive. This was all that was needed to confirm her suspicions. "Upon my soul, Rick! You have met Mary of Montlaine, haven't you?"

He was astonished. "What... how...?"

"Stupid! I was the one who first saw her. Don't you remember my telling you about a girl in the woods? Did you think I just let it go?"

"I... I didn't think about... I..."

"Well, I didn't let it go. I discussed it with Guss, as you might have realized I would."

"So... you know... about Mary... being here?"

"I do."

"And you have made no push to see her... talk with her?"

"No. It is not my place to intrude upon her privacy, is it?" She didn't say that she had been avoiding meeting Mary because she was afraid she might be tempted

126

to reassure the girl about her brother's safety.

"But . . . you still don't understand," he said on a note of despair.

"Lady Penrod is keeping her safely tucked away, Rick . . . doesn't that suggest to you that there is more to all this than meets the eye? How can you say *I* don't understand? Isn't it obvious to you what is at stake here?"

"Nessie . . . Mary thinks that the Echworths planned her brother's ruin!"

"Ah . . . does she?"

"You aren't shocked?"

"The possibility is a strong one, Rick."

"No . . . Sheila . . . Mrs. Echworth . . . couldn't . . . and even Orson . . . he isn't up to such treachery . . . such scheming . . . ?"

"That is the rub. They don't appear to have the cunning that must have been needed to plan such an involved deed."

"Ness . . . something must be done for Mary. She can't go on like this."

"Something will be done. Make yourself easy, Rick." She patted his arm. There was little else she could do for him now. She had her own fears to cope with.

Still in the cellar at Montlaine stood Epps, shuffling his feet and avoiding Orson Echworth's eye.

"Well . . . what in hell are you doing down here?" snapped Orson.

"There was a time when we kept some extra lumber 'ere, sir . . . I 'ad a notion to do a bit of repairing and only coome down . . ."

"And did you find the lumber?" interrupted Orson impatiently.

"No, I canna think whot becoome of it . . ."

127

"Well, never mind it now. It's late and you shouldn't be here."

"Aye, sir," said Epps, hurriedly ambling out.

Echworth watched him go, and there was a frown on his face. He didn't believe for a minute that Epps had been looking for lumber. But what then had Epps been doing in the cellar? He would have to watch this man more closely, and as soon as the estate was turned over to his family, he would dismiss the man!

The viscount hauled his supplies to his cave, dropping them with a heavy thud and startling his horse into a soft whinny.

"Hush, Midnight," he ordered in an irritated tone. His temper was strangely frayed. In answer the stallion put up his head alertly and backed up a pace. He sensed his master's mood and awaited the outcome.

The viscount chose to pace. He envisioned Vanessa in *his* dining room, in his library, flirting with Orson. For some reason, this was unpardonable. Here he had been, alone, waiting hopefully, expecting her to visit, while away his boredom, and where had she been? Dallying with the enemy!

She was a spoiled chit, and what she needed was a lesson! She had to be taught she couldn't play fast and loose with him! The irrationality of this did not occur to him, and within a space of moments he had worked a bit into his horse's mouth, flung on his flat saddle and jumped nimbly onto his horse's back. He took Midnight over the moors, across the field, through the Penrod thickets, and during that time allowed himself but one thought—Vanessa, naughty Vanessa, needed a lesson!

Thus driven, he secured his horse in the dark woods bordering the park and stood. How the deuce was he to know which room had been allocated to Vanessa? The house plan was well known to him, but this still was a problem.

He skirted the walls of the great house, attempting a process of elimination, when luck, ever a fickle seductress, winked his way. Lady Vanessa took her candleholder and opened her terrace door. She stood, the candlelight flickering over her alluring form as she gazed out on the night sky. The mist had finally withered, and the sky gave promise of a better day to come on the morrow. A breeze played with her long auburn hair, softly rustled her nightdress and then snuffed her candle. She sighed and moved within.

He smiled to himself, and with an excitement that set every nerve fiber tingling he set out to gain his ground. No rose trellis offered itself. No sturdy tree. How then to maneuver this fifteen-foot climb? It was then he saw the drainpipe. His smile curved into a grin. The lead pipe was strong enough to take his weight, and gripping it tightly he used it and the wall to get to his objective, the terrace. However, there was some distance between the drainpipe and the terrace ledge. He stretched out a long leg, pushed forward and found himself hanging onto the stone balustrade. Here he caught his breath and then hoisted himself up and over onto the terrace.

Within, Vanessa was in bed. Her eyes were closed and she was making a worthy attempt at sleep, but it would not come. A noise brought her head up. Another brought her hand to her covers, and unlike many a maid she did not dive beneath. Off they came. Instinct told her to be wary. Swiftly she crossed the room and flattened herself against the wall flanking her terrace door. Beside her hand she found an elegant china vase and thought it prudent to pick it up.

The viscount of Montlaine stepped quietly into the lady's chambers. He did not sneak, though he hoped his steps would not be detected as he moved toward her bed. Behind him, the lady did slink, raising the vase as high as she could and finding that if he did not bend, she would greatly miss her mark.

As he came upon the bed the moonlight caught the white of the sheets, and he discovered it to be empty. A sudden sense whirled him around, and there stood Vanessa, vase above her lovely head. His lips quivered.

She gasped, nearly screamed and stifled herself. One hand hugged the vase to her heart, the other waved at him in the dark. "Good gracious! You frightened me."

He looked at the vase and threw his cloak back over his shoulder as he spoke so that she had an excellent vision of his bronzed chest in the open-necked white shirt he wore. "Did I? You seemed well prepared nonetheless."

She laughed and put the vase away. "Yes, and so let that be a lesson to you before you go sneaking into a maiden's room at this time of night!"

"Tell me, would you have actually brought that down on my head, had you the opportunity?"

She shrugged. "I don't know . . . it would have been easier to shoot you I think, but as I didn't have a gun handy . . . But my lord, tell me, that is not why you are here. What is towards?" Then a frightened look leapt into her glance. "You are all right? No one has discovered you?"

He was surprised by the evident sincerity of her concern.

"Rest easy. As far as I know . . . I am still dead."

She frowned. "Then . . . why have you come here? This is madness. You might have been seen. Where is Midnight?"

130

"I was not seen, and Midnight is secure. I came..."
Now he was frowning. "....because..." He let go a
sigh. "The devil is in it that I don't know why I came!
Damnation, woman, why did you lead me to think you
would visit me this night if you knew you had plans
to dine with the Echworths at Montlaine?"

She saw the glitter in his black eyes. Such dark eyes,
wild and full with depths she wanted to explore, but
not now, not here. "My lord...I did not say I would
come to you. In fact, as I remember, you refused to
invite me to return." She wanted to tease him into a
better mood.

"I did not forbid you to come."

"It doesn't signify." She was moving away from him.
"I was obliged to attend your cousin's dinner...and
besides, I had nothing to report to you...the weather
kept me indoors all day."

He was hurt. It was ridiculous, but her coldness cut
through him almost savagely. The other night he had
been drawn to her, felt she was a kindred spirit. Now
she seemed to be throwing cold water at his face. What
was this Lady Vanessa that she would give nothing of
herself? Is that what she was doing? Withdrawing? So
be it. He made her a bow.

"I believe I was mistaken in you, my lady. I make
you my apologies for interrupting your rest." He
started across the room.

What was wrong? She was behaving like some missish ninny playing at love games. Why was she turning
him up cold? Why was she pushing him away? She
moved forward and blocked his path.

"Tell me, my lord...if I had come to you tonight
without anything new to advise you, what, just what,
would you have thought? What would you have done?"
She was trying to make a point. It misfired.

He looked at her then. She was the most beautiful woman he had ever known. Her gray sparkling eyes were full with life, hinting at passion secure in their inner regions. Her lips were full, cherry-red and inviting. Her skin was made to be touched, silky, yielding beneath his reaching hand.

"*This,* my lady." His voice was nearly a growl, so intense was his purpose.

His hand had taken her to him, pressed her against his hard lean body. His other hand had found the thickness of her long auburn hair, held it up to her shoulder as he bent her to his embrace. His mouth discovered hers in hungry need, softened into tenderness, sweetened into passion.

She came up from his kiss breathless, weak, and terribly, terribly afraid of what he had aroused within her breast. She had to get control of herself. Somehow she had to fend this rogue off before he made her his victim! Her voice? Where was her voice? Finally she managed in a shaky tone, "Precisely. So then, now you can go." She hated herself for speaking this way. Why, why was she doing it?

He was furious. "Is it only safe to do your teasing when you are in a drawing room? Does this bedroom...does my cave make you aware of what you really are...a thrill seeker?"

She cringed beneath the sting. Was it true? She felt his words, the tone of his voice, pierce her heart with their sharpness. Is that what he saw, an adventuress, a tease? Is that what she was? Her eyes were wild brilliant stars, glistening with hot flames in their centers. It wasn't so! Not with him...it hadn't been that way. She thought they had struck up a friendship. A tear escaped, wandered over her dark long lashes and fell upon her cheek. A sob threatened deep in her throat, but she checked it, and her voice came on a whisper.

"Your behavior makes me all too aware of what *you* think I am." She turned away from him. "I was wrong in you. I thought you knew better. Now if you don't mind, I... I want you to leave me alone."

He was upset with himself for behaving the frustrated cad. Her kiss had taken him to new realms never before explored, and had excited an all-new sensation. Her eyes had begged for his touch, teased for that kiss. What had gone wrong? Why had he given her such a setdown? What had made him say such a thing to her?

He had no immediate answer, so in silence he left the way he had come, and Lady Vanessa went to her bed, charged her pillow with some force and proceeded to cry herself into a state of fatigue.

Morning, clear, crisp, sweetly scented with summer blooms. However, it was wasted on the two young gentlemen meandering through Penrod Park.

Randall of Southvale turned his cousin around by his shoulders and stood his ground. "Imperative, Rick... absolutely imperative that we leave here at once!"

"Don't be a noddy," returned Richard on a sigh. "We can't."

"Must. Write to your father... tell him..."

"Tell him what?"

"That things are havey-cavey at Penrod. Won't like that. He'll want us to leave... see if he won't."

"'Havey-cavey'? That's famous," snickered Richard, but he was beginning to feel uneasy. What had gotten into his cousin?

133

"Rick . . . Rick . . . I saw her!"

"You saw who?"

"The girl in the cupboard."

"The girl in the cupboard? Have you gone daft?"

"You know I haven't. What's more, you know who I mean. I'm not needle-witted, never have been . . . but I know what I saw, know what I heard, and it's all too smoky by half. Pack up your sister and take her back to Brighton. Only reasonable thing to do."

"You've gone noddy on me, Rand. What are you talking about?" returned Richard warily.

His cousin lowered his voice. "Look here, Rick . . . the thing is she didn't mean for me to see her. 'Tis none of my affair if Lady Penrod chooses to hide girls in her cupboard and if you choose to play your games, but if Ness gets mixed up in this muddle, Uncle will have both our heads!"

"What makes you think Ness will get involved?"

"What makes you think Ness won't?" he returned knowingly.

"We can't go home. Randall . . . you don't understand."

"I understand we are slipping into something better left alone. Rick . . . the Echworths are searching for their niece . . . Lady Penrod told them she wasn't here . . . but she is . . . and she is hiding in the cupboard!" It was a desperate sound that Randy made.

Richard of Grey let go a long sigh. "How do you know that?"

"Who else could the girl be? And it's no use saying you know naught about the affair when it was you she was calling this morning!"

"What? Explain yourself," returned Rick, giving nothing away that he needn't.

"I was in the library, relaxing with my coffee, when

134

at my back I hear, 'Psst...Richard...psst.' Well, I turned around, only natural thing to do. There she was, this little bit of fluff, she lets go a scream and dives behind the cupboard and vanishes. I tell you frankly, Rick...I don't like it!"

Ricky let go an exasperated sigh. "It's our hair...she must have mistook you for me from the back...though I can't see it. My shoulders are broader and I am taller..."

"You are not!" Randall pulled himself up to his full height and puffed out his chest.

"Yes I am..."

"Turn about, I say!" raged Randall of Southvale. "Come on...back to back!"

"Don't be a noddy. Anyway, this is getting us nowhere. We must think of something!"

"Go home. Only thing to do," returned his cousin, applying himself once more to the problem at hand.

"That's a poor-spirited thing to suggest. The girl is in trouble, Randy....Do you mean to leave her to fend for herself?"

"Not my affair. Not your affair...Uncle wouldn't want it to be. You've a bit more bottom than sense, Rick...only do but think! Lady Penrod is harboring the Montlaine chit here in secret...it's bound to rake up a scandal in the end. No place for Ness to be. Your father won't want her involved."

Richard reflected upon this a moment and shook his head. "It don't involve Ness. Ain't her establishment. What Lady Penrod does ain't Ness's affair!"

"Famous! You are sticking your head in the sand. Ness is bound to make the entire thing her affair in the end. I tell you there is something smoky afoot...can't put m'finger on it but know that all is not what it seems."

"You are right there!"

"And a rare set-to there will be in the end with Ness's name bandied about. Mark me, Richard," said his cousin gravely, "you are serving your sister an ill turn if you allow her to remain here."

Richard of Grey frowned. "Thing is . . . she won't go either, Rand. There is no way that I can force her . . . and truth is I wouldn't even if I could. Mary is in trouble . . . and Lady Penrod just isn't the one to handle this any more."

"And *you* think yourself qualified to take over?" returned his cousin depressingly.

"A sight more than her ladyship is. Lord, Randall, you don't think I am going to allow that poor child to be thrown to the dogs?"

"I can hardly consider the Echworths quite in that light, old boy . . . can you?"

"Yes . . . no . . . damn if I know. Look here, cuz . . . Mary fears them, she thinks they did her brother harm for the inheritance and that they won't stop until they have it all, which means they must dispose of her. Lady Penrod must have her fears on the same grounds if she is willing to keep the child in hiding."

"Then there is only one solution, Rick. Surprised you didn't think of it." He shook his head sadly. "Tricky . . . but the only real answer. Think it will serve . . ."

"What in thunder are you babbling about? Come on, Randall, spit it out."

"Send Mary to the Echworths. Be on guard. They wouldn't dare have a go at her with all eyes upon them."

For a long moment Richard of Grey did not trust himself to comment. He stared with utter disbelief be-

136

fore the explosion came. "You are mad! You are saying we should set the child up as bait?"

"Think on it, Rick ... bound to work ..."

"Plague take you for a halfwit!" returned his cousin before stalking off back in the direction of the house.

Chapter Twelve

Lady Vanessa's eyes showed evidence of strain. Her hair, though silky with its natural shine, was not as carefully dressed as usual and hung about her shoulders indifferently. Her habit, though, was as always in perfect style. A top hat of dark-green silk sat jauntily upon her well-shaped head. A matching dark-green jacket fit closely over her white lacy blouse. The dark-green skirt fell neatly over her graceful height as she descended the stairs. Her animation, though, seemed still abed until she caught sight of her brother slamming the front doors.

"Richard!" she called in some astonishment.

He cast his eyes up at her and returned, "Come down to the library. I want to have a word with you."

She raised one fine brow but said nothing as she proceeded to do his bidding. Once alone with him in the library she set down her light kid gloves and sighed.

"Now, if you please, why are you behaving like a little boy who has just been beaten at cricket?"

"Stop it, Ness! This is no funning matter, and I am dead serious."

"Ah, I can see that you are."

"Randall has seen Mary and means for us to leave Penrod. Has it in his head *you* are bound to get mixed up in the affair and end in another scrape. I am worried that he might take it upon himself to write to Father."

Lady Vanessa sat down upon the nearest chair and let go a small cry. "*No!* Oh, Rick . . . Rick . . . I can't . . . won't go . . ."

He looked at her strangely. "I didn't think so . . . but Ness . . . how deeply are you involved in this?"

She controlled herself cautiously. "Involved? I don't know what you mean."

"Don't you, my girl? Somehow I don't think you're telling me true. Come on then, Ness . . . are you playing me false in this?"

"How can you say such a thing to me?" She shook her head, avoiding his eyes. "I care . . . certainly I care about the Montlaine name . . . about your young friend Mary . . ."

He sighed and took a turn of the room. "What is to be done, then?"

"What exactly did Randy say?"

"Wants to hand Mary over to the Echworths . . . says we'll flush them out. The lad is quite out, of course."

"Rick . . . our cousin does have something of a notion there."

"Burn it, girl, you can't mean that?" he asked incredulously.

"Only do think. If we were to tell the Echworths that Mary has returned to Penrod . . . that she is still in a decline over her brother's death, that she would rather stay at Penrod than return to the memories at Montlaine . . . ?"

"Dash it, Ness . . . I won't risk it!"

"But I will!" returned a small voice.

Two pairs of eyes turned to find Mary of Montlaine clothed in bright-yellow muslin closing the secret panel door at her back and stepping into the warmth of the library. Richard of Grey stepped forward and took up her hands. "Mary . . . you cannot mean it!"

"Oh, but I do." She looked up into his deep-blue eyes, and saw there concern and warmth, and thus encouraged she continued, "If we are to flush out the Echworths and clear my brother's name, we have to give them space and purpose. I will be perfectly safe . . . with *you* to watch over me."

Vanessa was not surprised by the girl's obvious faith in her brother. Clearly, Mary of Montlaine was infatuated with Richard. She studied instead with some interest her brother's reaction to all this. Richard was frowning at the pretty dark-haired young thing. He seemed absorbed with her nearly black eyes, but he had not the look of a man in love. Ah, poor child, thought Vanessa. "We cannot depend solely on Richard's powers of protection, Mary. There is a great deal of danger involved. First of all, we cannot be certain the Echworths were behind your brother's troubles. Someone else might have . . ."

"There is no one else. Only Duncan and Orson hated my brother, wished him ill . . . and really stood to gain," she returned.

Vanessa was struck in that moment by the girl's likeness to her brother. She had not his height, for she was petite in figure, and her features too were finer, more chiseled, but there was a tone of voice, an expression of countenance, a style of movement, and the words spilled out before she realized them. "My . . . you are so much like your brother . . ."

"Am I?" The girl beamed. "But . . . did you know Bret?"

Vanessa bit her lip. "No...unfortunately...but there is the portrait of him at Montlaine," she put in lamely.

"Oh yes..." the girl's expression softened. "You would have liked him."

"I am sure."

"Let us get back to the business at hand, Ness. You must convince Mary that all this is wild talking."

"I am afraid I cannot do that, Richard. Only do but consider. Eventually, Mary will have to be returned to her home and her guardian, Duncan Echworth. Would you not rather she is presented to them while *we* are at Penrod? Would you not rather that she remains at Penrod for the summer...with us? In truth, she will be safer here with us whoever the culprit is."

"Your sister is right. You know that she is, so don't be difficult, Richard," put in Mary.

He shuffled his feet to this, but seemed disinclined to respond. Vanessa sighed. "Well...talk it over with Lady Penrod, won't you? I must go now."

"Go? You can't go," returned Richard.

"I have an errand that cannot wait." And with this she waved herself off.

In exasperation Richard turned his eyes toward Mary, who beamed at him. "Richard, only think...once we have told them all I am here, we can go about the countryside together. I will show you Cornwall!"

"Egad!" responded Lord Richard of Grey.

At Montlaine two figures strolled side by side. The girl from a distance appeared angelic in her flowing white muslin gown. The wind whipped at her loose ginger locks, and her hand moved to catch a strand and tuck it in behind her ear. Her face arched to give her companion a coy inviting eye.

Edward Parks bent, picked a white rose and handed it to her with a warm smile. She accepted it, put it to her nose and gurgled with laughter. "Ah, my staid Edward. You are disapproving still."

"And should I not be after the manner in which you conducted yourself last evening?"

She put up her chin. "Don't be nonsensical. Those boys are naught to me . . . and if they will pay me court, 'tis not my fault, after all . . . is it?"

"Isn't it? You encouraged them, Sheila." He seemed very jealous indeed.

She clapped her hands together. "You are mad with jealously! Ah, but this is marvelous. My quiet Edward, moved to such passion."

He took her shoulders, and there was an angry glint in his blue eyes. "Am I? I am afraid you miss the point, Sheila my love." He released her then and said more quietly, "The question is, should I be?"

She smiled. She was not in love with Edward Parks, but this was great fun. Furthermore, it gave her something of a perverse pleasure to have Edward Parks in her hand. He had been a close friend to the late viscount. She hated the viscount of Montlaine, and burning his friend, as she intended burning Edward Parks, was a delightful prospect. "You needn't be . . . if you behave yourself, dearest Edward."

"And have I not been behaving myself?" He tilted his head as he spoke, giving an inflection to his tone that she could not mistake.

"Yes, but you are too slow." She pouted.

"What I need is for you to draw up exactly what you would like and I shall have the papers ready for your brother's signature upon his return," said Edward Parks.

"But I have already told you . . ." she complained.

"That is not good enough, my dear. Orson says one thing, you another."

"Orson? What has he to say to anything? You are not helping him, but me!"

"Orson has made me an interesting offer, love . . ."

She came closer, and meaningfully she put her body against his. "And I have not?"

"In this, we will do it my way. I am no fool, Sheila. In your next missive to me, you will outline the text of your agreement with Duncan. I will then draw up the papers and present it to him for his signature . . . after he has agreed, of course."

"He will sign. It is in your hands, Edward . . . for if you manage to do the little favor he wants, he will be happy to give over the little that I ask. He is not mean-fisted, after all."

"Is he not?" Edward Parks smiled ruefully. "Well, we shall see." He hesitated a moment. Watching her face brought back a memory, and he could not refrain from saying, "Now and then I marvel at your bitterness against the late viscount, Sheila. There was a time when . . . when I was certain you held him in great esteem."

"Did you think that? Well . . . evidently you were wrong. Duncan told me what he was . . . Duncan knew he would end in wickedness, and so he did."

"You admire your brother Duncan?"

"I adore him. Who would not? And Duncan has such powers . . ."

"Powers? What sort of powers?"

"Never mind. He will be home soon enough, and see if things don't run smoothly then." She put her arms around Edward Parks's neck and whispered teasingly, "Now, Edward . . . show me just how much you want me."

"Sheila...we are in full view of the house."

She pulled away and pulled a grimace. "You are rude, Edward...and staid...all too staid. Perhaps I shall not deal with you after all?"

He turned her to him and sighed. "You will end in ruining us both, my girl." With this he obeyed her earlier command.

When he released her she let go a small laugh, touched his lip and said quietly, "My poor Edward..."

Bess Widdons was a tall girl whose unwieldy form had never softened into grace. Her limbs were thin and too long, her features were gaunt, her nose sharp, and her eyes, which could have been her finest point, were too often veiled in wistful sadness. Her address was quiet, shrinking, and with good reason. Her appearance had often made her the object of hurtful jests. Even so, an onlooker would point out that she was a princess in her father's world. A successful world, financially, offering her much that a maid could want.

Her father, Henry Widdons, prided himself on his mill, his home and his family—much in that order. His mill had grown and now lay in a horseshoe pattern around a house that had steepled from a one-room cottage to a three-story structure. How often he sighed happily and praised the Lord he had instituted the use of the Cartwright's wool-combing machine. Herein lay his success. It had enabled him to provide his family with the things he had always prized and never had when he had been a lad. Why, hadn't he sent his daughter to the finest finishing school in all of England?

In answer, Bess Widdons would have nodded dutifully, much as she always did whenever he chanced to pose such a question. She hadn't been happy there, but he never asked about that. Do not mistake, it wasn't because he didn't care, it was because it never entered his mind that such a possibility existed, and she never cared to spoil his dream. She hadn't belonged to that world. She was the daughter of a tradesman in a school filled with the spoiled beauties of aristocracy. She was the butt of their jests. She was their scapegrace; never did any one of them choose her for friend.

Smile, Bess, smile! Every now and then he would catch her expression and frown as he bellowed this command. She would try and he would grin and exclaim it was time she had a new gown. Yes, she had many lovely things, and now she no longer fit in with the girls she had grown up with. She was caught in a limbo world, neither here nor there. Only Melony had wanted her for friend. Only Melony had taken the trouble to look past the unattractive face and find something worthy of friendship. How she had loved Melony Fry . . . and now she was gone.

She stopped her steps upon the dirt road and bent to take up some heather. Melony had loved the heather. She breathed the scent in deeply, saw the breeze play with the wild daisies and nearly went off again into tears. She was always crying these days. So much had happened. Everything was so miserably complicated, and life was once again tinged with loneliness.

Lady Vanessa took the bend in the road carelessly as her horse switched leads. It left her panting and laughing a bit as she slid forward on the saddle. "Ho there, Shadow . . . silly mare . . . ho before I fall off!" She brought her up sharply and sat a moment taking in air. It was then she saw Bess Widdons standing to the side of the road looking up at her with something of awe in her expression.

"Oh . . . hallo, I do hope I didn't startle you."

146

There was a friendliness in the smile that cowered Bess into shyness. "No . . . well, only a little . . . she is lovely, your horse."

"Why, yes, I think so too, how kind of you to agree." It was Ness's humor, but it set the girl to blushing. Ness was surprised and nimbly jumped off her horse with the intention of setting the girl at her ease. "I am Lady Vanessa . . . staying with Lady Penrod at the Tower. I am just on my way to visit with Bess Widdons. I do hope I am on the right road . . . I wasn't quite certain back at the fork." She had turned in the direction she had just come from. With her words she returned her attention back to the girl towering above her own ample height and was surprised to see the girl's countenance lose all color.

"But . . . why . . . why are you looking for *me?*"

"Oh, are you Miss Widdons? How very pleased I am to find you at last. I waited an age for you the other day . . . did no one tell you?"

"Y-es . . . they mentioned something about it . . . but . . . I don't understand what *you* could want with me?" There was a frightened inflection in the girl's voice.

"Well, you needn't look like that, I shan't eat you." Vanessa smiled kindly. "I came only to talk with you . . . about a matter that is extremely delicate and confidential."

The girl frowned. "But . . . I don't know anything."

"Now, I am certain that you do know a great many things, so that is a singularly odd thing to say," bantered Vanessa, hoping to mitigate the girl's apprehension.

This did in fact bring a smile to Bess's lip, and Vanessa cooed softly, cajolingly, "There, I made certain you had a lovely smile and I was right. Now then, do you think we could discuss my problem now . . . while we walk together? Or would you prefer to return to your house for our chat?"

Lady Vanessa's poise, her stature, her beauty, were at once to a girl of Bess Widdon's stamp awe-inspiring, yet she found Vanessa of Grey uniquely different from ladies of her set. For one thing, her directness was a thing she found both intriguing and alarming. She was therefore still much on her guard when she responded that she would rather they conduct their talk right where they were.

Lady Vanessa did a quick study of the girl's face. There was much going on in this chit's head, and a great deal of it pulled at Ness's soft heart. She reached out reassuringly and patted the girl's arm. "I think perhaps the matter I am about to broach to you may be . . . painful, and I want you to know now that if it is, I am sorry for it. You will, I believe, forgive me when you understand the reasons for my questions."

"Questions? What then do you want to know?"

"I am here because of Mary of Montlaine . . . no, please don't turn away."

"I was not acquainted with the poor girl," said Bess. She kept her face averted, for the memories of the last few months began to flood into her head.

"No . . . but you were, I understand, a good friend of Melony Fry's?"

The girl gasped. "Who . . . who told you that?"

"Never mind . . . isn't it true?"

"Yes, yes it is true, and I am proud of it!"

"Faith, child . . . why shouldn't you be?" returned Vanessa, her own delicate brows drawing together. Here was something unexpected.

Bess blushed hotly and turned away. Her voice was low, muffled.

"My father did not approve of my friendship with Melony. We had always to meet in secret. It was of course, ridiculous. We had known each other all our lives."

"Why didn't he wish you to continue your friendship with her? Had she done something he could not like?"

"No...oh no...Father never knew. You see, Father has great plans for me. He wanted me to mix with girls...better equipped financially..."

"I see, but you said...your father never knew. Never knew what?" pursued Vanessa carefully.

"Why are you asking me all these questions? Why do you want to know about my friendship with Melony?"

"Because not long ago the viscount of Montlaine suffered an accusation that led to his death and the ruin of his family name. No one tried to clear him, and now his sister carries the burden. I am trying to get at the truth."

"I...I can't help you."

"But Bess...you can if you will." She reached out to halt the girl, for Bess began to walk away in her agitation. "No, don't run away from me. Melony was...if we are to believe the good vicar...involved in a demon's cult. Did you know about it?"

"Yes! Yes...as I was!" The girl began to sob then, and Vanessa put an arm about her waist. "Oh, my lady...I have kept it to myself...for so long... we...I didn't know how it would turn out. I never believed in what we were doing...it was just a lark...nothing more than a lark...and then Melony told me that the master...that she and he...had become lovers..."

"Who was the master?" Lady Vanessa asked the question, and while she waited for the answer she tensed.

149

"I don't know. At first she used to tease me and say he was Montlaine... who else did I think he was? we all thought him the viscount... all the other girls still do... but they weren't friends of Melony's... they didn't know."

"Didn't know what?"

"That... that she was carrying the master's child!" She covered her face with her hands. "Oh... please... please... you mustn't tell my father... it would break his heart... he wants so much for me..."

"Hush, child... your father needn't know... let us hope he need never know about your part in the cult. Only you must tell me all you know. Obviously Melony knew who the master was. Didn't she confide in you?"

"No. She couldn't. She said if she did it might prove to be dangerous for me. She was desperately in love with him... and afraid of him as well."

"What makes you think he wasn't the viscount of Montlaine?"

"Oh... I don't know exactly... some of the things she said... and then finally when she told him she was carrying his child, he treated her badly. She told me he said he wouldn't marry her, that he wouldn't let her stand in his way." She sucked in air and caught her breath. "Lady Vanessa... she was in a rage, and she told me that she intended to ruin his plans if he would not marry her."

"She said that? Ruin his plans?"

"Exactly. That is another reason that made me think he was not Montlaine... that and of course the way she flirted with Montlaine whenever he chanced to pass her in the fields."

"What do you mean?"

"Well... he would pass us now and then... on that black stallion of his... and he would stop and dally with Melony. She always enjoyed that, but there was nothing intense about it. With the master she behaved quite differently ... almost worshipfully. Oh, the master had her quite in his power."

"And this master ... did he come to the cult meetings on a black stallion?"

"That is another thing ... he did ride a black horse. It could have been a stud ... but there was something different about his horse. He didn't have the same strong lines of Midnight. Oh, I just don't know."

Vanessa nibbled at her fingertip thoughtfully. "Bess ... Melony did say she would tell him she was going to ruin his plans? She didn't say she would expose him to the village for his demonology?"

"No ... not expose him ... she said she would ruin his plans. She told him that and he asked for time ... he used it to ... to ..."

Lady Vanessa patted her hand, and gently she asked, "Knowing all this, Bess ... you kept quiet?"

"How could I know the village would march against Montlaine? It happened all so quickly. I was closeted in my room ... so very upset about Melony, you see. I loved her ... she was my only friend. By the time I discovered ... well ... by that time the viscount had already gone over the cliff. There was no sense in my coming forward with my suspicions then. To what purpose? I had only speculation to propose, and I did not want my father humiliated by the discovery of my past conduct as a cult member."

Vanessa could have stamped her vexation. "But surely, Bess, you could recognize his voice?"

Bess shook her head. "I don't know that I could. You see, he always took such care to muffle it behind that black mask he wore. He disguised its tone so that nearly every time he spoke he used a different inflection. He never came very close to any of us . . . he never went into the cirle of fire. I just don't see how any of this will help clear the name of Montlaine."

"Don't you, Bess? You said you had your suspicions. I have my own, but more than that, I strongly believe you know who the master was."

"I don't! I swear it! Please, Lady Vanessa . . . I don't." There was fear in the girl's eyes.

Vanessa pushed for home. "Bess . . . don't you see, if we believe Montlaine was innocent, then you must realize the man who decreed Melony's death is still walking freely about."

"I have told you all I know . . . no . . . let me go . . . I have to go home."

Vanessa let go of the girl's arm. She could see that Bess was too frightened to say any more just now. Perhaps later after some soul-searching Bess might be willing to say more.

"Thank you, Bess. Perhaps I may yet use what you have told me to ferret out our demon."

Bess frowned. "I don't know that you should, my lady . . . he is dangerous. But believe me, I wish you may." She began to move away, stopped and turned. "I am sorry I couldn't tell you more, and you will remember to keep your promise. My father . . . he mustn't know . . . he would never understand."

"I'll remember," said Vanessa, but as Bess Widdons moved out of sight she frowned worriedly. In truth she wasn't sure just how to use what she had learned.

Chapter Thirteen

The viscount of Montlaine had not returned that same night to his cave dwelling. Instead he rode his horse hard and recklessly over the dark moors until he found himself heading in the direction of his friend. It was then he made a decision. With a grim face he continued until he reached Edward Parks's grounds. There he quietly attended to his horse, stabled the stallion and made his way to his friend's window. There he maintained his composure as he once again scaled the walls to Parks's open window.

Unsuspecting, Edward lay sleeping soundly in his bed. Observing this, the viscount's lips twitched and some of his humor returned to him. He bent and gave Edward's shoulder a vigorous shake.

"Edward! Come on, you old dog! Wake up!"

Edward groaned and attempted to roll over. This was foiled, however, as the viscount yanked off the covers and gave his closest friend a swift shove. "Edward, I say!"

"Huh? Go away...oh, please, Bret...do go away..."

Edward was roused to plead, whereupon he buried his face into his pillow.

Montlaine let go a short laugh. "Up, Edward! You lead too easy a life. It has made you soft." He tossed the blankets off his friend and pulled out the pillow so that Parks fell flat upon his mattress.

"Plague take you!" Edward was moved to cry as he rose to a sitting position and rubbed the sleep from his eyes. "What in thunder are you about at this hour?"

Montlaine's lips formed a sneer, and Edward was struck by the satanic aura of his friend's countenance. At moments like this it was easy to see how things had gotten out of hand.

"Edward, the time has come to end the sort of life I have been living, if life it has been. I plan to go this afternoon to the magistrate and request a trial by my peers!"

Edward was on his feet immediately. "Thunder and turf, man, do you realize what you are saying?"

"Do you think I don't?" He put his hand through his hair and paced. "Damnation! We have made absolutely no progress. At least if I were out in the open . . ."

"You would be out in the open, no more. You think that would serve?"

"Perhaps."

His friend shot him a crushing glance. "Don't be absurd! What has put you in such a taking I don't know, and at just this time. Plague take it, Bret, I didn't want you to know . . . for you are bound to make all sorts of objections we can ill afford to consider . . . but as I am making some headway . . ."

"Will you stop prosing on and on and tell me what in blazes you are talking about?" put in the viscount impatiently.

"I have been courting your cousin, my friend. I hope you won't mind," returned Edward nonchalantly.

"Have you, by Jupiter?" retorted the viscount disbelievingly. "I felicitate you. Now, will you be serious?"

"Oh, but I am, Bret. I am instantly transported at the very mention of my darling Sheila's name," returned Edward Parks on a grave note.

The viscount studied him a moment and then let go a shout of laughter. "Stap me if you didn't almost have me believe you."

Edward Parks feigned hauteur. "Pray, sir, why wouldn't you believe me?"

"Cut line dog! Now, what is all this about you and Sheila? For I tell you frankly, Edward, the chit means mischief, and if she has been casting out lures your way I'd be wary."

Edward put up a finger. "I find your remark vastly interesting, for that is precisely what Sheila had done. Now, naturally being a charming fellow I could have easily supposed the maid had been captivated by my extraordinary good looks and delightful wit. Alas, I am something of a cynic and decided to look further."

"And?"

"And have come up with but one conclusion. I needs must sweep the maid off her feet and make her mine," rallied Parks.

"To what purpose?" The viscount had moved forward on his chair.

"Aha, I see that although you ask, you really already know, don't you?"

"I think so, but Edward, this is dangerous . . . *for you.*"

"Is it? I don't think so . . . only hear what I have discovered and how much more we have to gain."

The telling of this particular tale took some time and thorough exploration by both men, and it was not until the wee hours of the morning that the viscount took to his allotted quarters.

Montlaine's dreams when sleep finally overtook were frenzied, garbled and threaded with terrors that men falter to admit. Even so when he awoke at last the first thought that came brought with it a vision. Bright silvery eyes danced in a countenance full with mischief and feminine charm. Vanessa! Damn, what had she to do with him now? Vanessa. The viscount of Montlaine released a heavy sigh.

It was past noon when the viscount finally rose from his bed and found that his friend had already departed to court the fair Sheila. It was also just about that hour when an interesting development shook the house of Montlaine.

Edward Parks had just left Sheila and therefore missed the arrival of Duncan Echworth. A hired post chaise slowly came to a stop before the great doors of Montlaine Castle. Duncan Echworth stepped forth and was ushered within. He was received with polite reverence by the servants, for he was the heir. His presence among them was the cause of backstairs disturbance and conjecture, much of this having to do with his appearance. It was always so when they gazed upon the Echworth brothers. This because they were twins and so alike that rarely could they be seen together without setting the tongues to wagging.

Duncan stood beside his younger twin and saw his reflection. The servants as always were overawed by their remarkable likeness, but to the discerning eye there was a notable difference between the two brothers. Orson was known for his style of dress and his delicate mannerisms. From the top of his yellow hair to the tips of his shining Hessians, Orson was a dandy. He prided himself on his shirtpoints, on his intricate cravats, on the fit of his coats, on his style of address, and had in fact made quite a name for himself in the polite world.

Duncan was the elder twin, and while not a slovenly or unfashionable man, he rather despised foppery and never paid the cut of his coat much heed. He was a scamp forever in search of a jest, far too active, too playful, too much of a larkster to mind if his Hessians were scuffed or his cravat not quite as it should be. Orson would cluck his tongue at Duncan's mannerisms, and Duncan every bit the rogue cavalier, would laugh and make no attempt to curb his wayward temperment.

The twins found themselves, by select contrivance, within a short span of time quite private in the Montlaine library. So it was that the brothers considered one another, and one made the other an exaggerated bow.

"You are ... perfection itself. Indeed, Orson, I am thoroughly convinced that you can be none other than the *charming Duncan Echworth!*" He put both hands on his twin's shoulders and gave him an affectionate squeeze. "Did you play the part well?"

Orson Echworth had for the last few months been acting out a role. He had gone to London as Duncan Echworth. It had been an easy thing, for as youngsters they had often switched identities to play off a spoof against their cronies. This time, however, a different purpose had been behind the masquerade. Orson inclined his fair head.

"It will please you no end, Duncan ... but I have even added a few charmers to your long list of hearts, though in truth I found no pleasure in it. Women are all the same—tiresome creatures. What above the physical you find to so intrigue you is quite beyond my comprehension!"

"Ah, but the physical, Orson, you will admit, holds

157

the attention long enough," bantered his twin.

Orson was struck as always when in his twin's company by the charm of the deadly smile. Duncan was, had always been, the stronger one, the dominant force. Always Duncan had ruled. Orson felt bound to him in a way he had never understood. It was a troubling feature of their relationship. It was Duncan who would take command, and it was he who would meekly follow.

"Dash it, Duncan, I hope you managed to curtail that attitude while playing me?"

Duncan laughed. "Be easy, brother. I held myself in admirable check ... even when invited to waver I did not, and let me tell you, the temptation was as plump a chambermaid as ever I desired to pinch. But never mind, I looked the other way and behaved just as *you* would." He sighed and took a seat. "In fact, only one fair charmer deterred my purpose, but I shall set that to rights."

"Oh, now we are in for it. From the outset I knew this wouldn't work ..."

"Shut up, Orson. It has worked! Now hear me out. I have met a woman ... and how I chanced to overlook her during her London seasons amazes me ... but it doesn't matter, for I have found her and mean to have her."

"You ... you dallied with some wench when masquerading as me?" exploded his twin angrily. "Duncan ... I won't have it ... and if you mean for me to carry on with the charade ..."

"I don't! No, this wench I don't mean to share with anyone, not even with you. The staid and dandified Orson Echworth will lose interest in my beauty ... but her heart will not break, for Duncan will step in. You will introduce us this evening, in fact, for Mother and Sheila have wangled an invitation from Lady Penrod."

158

"Lady Penrod? Damnation. Who is this chit?"

"She is Lady Vanessa Grey," returned Duncan quietly.

"Good damn! Never say you mean to play with the house of Grey? Duncan ... this is folly!"

"Orson, you misunderstand. I mean to wed my beautiful heiress. Now that I have the title and the fortune, there can be no objection."

"No, Grey can make no objection to a Montlaine ... but Duncan, you haven't the title or the estate, and there is still Mary to be thought of," put in Orson gallingly. "After all, the plan was that you would wed her and thereby obtain the entire Montlaine fortune!"

Duncan frowned. "There are other ways of dealing with Mary and getting our hands on the Montlaine fortune without making the chit my wife! And by the by ... Parks means to throw in with us. He wants Sheila, and together they want a rather hefty sum. I have thought it over and believe I will allow him to aid us, for he means to lend a hand with regards to Mary." He sighed, but there was no sincerity in the concern he affected. "It is rather sad, though, for Sheila will soon have to look elsewhere for a husband. I don't mean to allow Parks to survive long enough to enjoy our money." There was a grim look about his mouth.

Orson was horrified. "Duncan ... you don't mean ... my God ... Duncan, that girl ... Melony ... her death ... do you mean ... you ... ?"

Duncan only smiled. "Don't concern yourself with such things, brother. You were never able to shoulder the realities of our hard lives. Do but leave those things to me."

Orson shuddered. "Do you know ... you are positively terrifying at times."

"Do you think so?" Duncan smiled and turned to

look up at the portrait of Montlaine. "It is a wonder *he* never took me seriously, but then he didn't know I had taken your place here and you mine in London. He never lit onto what I had in mind." He laughed, and his twin released yet another shudder.

The hour was late, and Lady Penrod's guests were due to arrive for dinner. Richard of Grey put the finishing pinch to his elegantly tied cravat and appraised the results in his long looking glass. His hair was suitably disarrayed, giving the appearance that he cared little for its style, when in reality its windswept achievement had taken no less than twenty minutes. His dark-green coat had been carefully selected to match his ivory silk waistcoat with its dark-green embroidery. His buff knit breeches fit his long slim legs, and he felt that all in all he made quite a favorable show. With a sigh of satisfaction he made his way down his hallway to a set of narrow winding stairs which led to Mary's tower room. There he found her oaken door and began pounding unceremoniously for admittance.

"Mary! Come on, girl . . . Mary . . ."

The door opened wide and Mary of Montlaine was roused to expostulate in awesome terms, "Richard . . . how grand you do look, why . . . *you are beautiful!*"

"Beautiful? You little wretch!" returned he. "You don't call a man beautiful." He moved within and did a turn about her, appraising her carefully, thoughtfully, with one finger to his lip. She appeared with her dark short curls and her dark eyes a veritable imp. Her figure, still youthful, had not filled out enough to match her mind, a fact that had brought the frown to her eyes only moments before. Her schooldress of white muslin made her appear all the more a child, but he was struck

160

by her prettiness all the same. "I say, Mary...you aren't looking half bad yourself... for a chit still in the schoolroom, that is."

She wanted to kick him. She settled for pulling a face, thought this not quite enough chastisement and followed it up by sticking her tongue out at him. "You are horrid, Richard. That is no way to speak to a woman you are escorting to dinner!"

"No, indeed... heaven forbid... but Mary, you ain't a woman, so don't fly into the boughs with me." He took her hand as though to mitigate the blow, and though she moved to pull it away he gripped it firmly and slid it through his crooked arm. "There now, don't be a brat of a chit. Chances are, you know, that you'll be a woman soon enough, Mary...and then wishing yourself a child." He heaved a sigh. "Now, once more before I take you downstairs, are you certain about this?"

Her little face took a grim expression and one beyond her years. "Yes, Richard, it must be done...you know that."

He was struck to the heart. He patted her small white hand.

"Well, you ain't lilly-livered. Pluck to the core. But the devil's in it, girl... this time I wish it weren't so."

"No, you don't mean that. You would be sadly disappointed in me if I were to turn missish and run," she retorted wisely.

He gave her a long admiring look. "Well then, brat, nothing for it but to head on!"

It was all happening so fast, thought Orson as he moved into the room. Here he was walking toward a woman he had never before met and having to pass through the ordeal. He could feel his hands trembling

161

as he clasped them behind his back.

"Lady Vanessa," he said, smiling at her. His voice came slowly, carefully. There was a studied quality to it. "I am pleased to present to you my brother . . . Duncan."

Lady Vanessa had been softly conversing with Lady Penrod when the Echworths were announced. Out of politeness she had gone with her cousin Randy to engage Sheila, as Mrs. Echworth's attention had been commanded by Lady Penrod. She turned to the sound of Orson's voice only to find lurking in the background another man she could not quite see, as he stood away from the glare of the candlelight and a shadow hid his features.

She listened to the introduction and glanced sharply at Orson a moment. There was something strangely odd . . . distant in his manner, so very much at variance with his earnest flirting of the other night. She looked past him with interest and was then astounded as Duncan Echworth moved forward.

Duncan took her hand. She was exquisite, more so every time he saw her anew. He was amused with the situation. He could see that his brother was apprehensive of this meeting. Didn't Orson realize by now just how much he could carry off? Well, if he didn't, he soon would.

"Enchanted, Lady Vanessa," he said to the accompaniment of a smooth smile. "My brother has told me so much about you that I feel already that we are acquainted."

Lady Vanessa attempted to bring her thoughts about. Here was Duncan Echworth. Twins! She had never thought of that. Twins. No one had ever mentioned it to her, and why it should send a rush of excitement through her was more than she could fathom.

There was something in it... something she just could not touch at the moment.

"I... er... rather feel the same way," she answered at last, noting that the curve of his lip reminded her exactly of the trick Orson had with his flitting expressions. "Please do excuse me... I must appear very stupid to you... it is just that I am overwhelmed at the likeness between you and your brother. No one ever mentioned to me that you two were twins."

He smiled benignly. "Most people find it disconcerting at first, but I fancy you have a discerning eye and will soon learn to tell us apart."

"Oh... I think you credit me with more discernment than I possess." Vanessa laughed.

"Do but consider the realities, Lady Vanessa. Look there at my brother, at his mode of dress, at his cool exterior. There stands every hostess's dream. The perfect gentlemen. Never flustered, always tasteful, always ready to do the correct thing at all social functions." He hesitated a fraction of a moment. "And now, my beauty, take appraisal of me." He waited for her to turn her critical eye upon his person. "That's right. I dress well enough... but nothing to denote the touch of Brummell about my person. I should always be invited to the season's routs, but note that mothers would steer their daughters clear of me..."

She laughed. "No, they would not! Mr. Echworth, may I remind you that you are soon to inherit an old and honorable title..."

"Ah yes, and the wealth to bear it up. So then, perhaps in the future mamas would push their daughters in my way, but I am a callous cavalier and would step over all but the most beautiful. My brother would be moved to mortification over such behavior."

"Stop. You paint a wicked picture indeed."

"But do you believe it?" He was suddenly very close to her. The sweet fragance of her person aroused him, and he wasn't sure how he would manage to keep from taking her up in his arms.

She gave him a measured look. "Yes, I think I do."

He put his finger to her chin. "Wise lady . . . but for *you* I shall endeavor to reform."

"Oh no. Do not even suggest such a thing. Why . . . women need men like you, Mr. Echworth. You are a supremely romantic figure who should never tie yourself to any one woman but should go on fanning the passions." She was bantering, attempting to keep their dallying light and airy.

He meant to steer her otherwise. "At the moment I can think of only one woman worth the bother . . ." His voice was low, soft with his meaning.

Lady Vanessa's seasons had prepared her for such behavior in men. She was rarely at a loss for a rebuke, but there was something in Duncan Echworth's address that frightened her a little. Then too she was still startled by the fact that they had only just met, and yet she had the feeling that she knew him rather well. This was, of course, she told herself, because of her acquaintance with Orson. Another oddity that nagged at her. Orson had only last night attempted to carry on a serious flirtation. Now, Orson seemed little interested in her or in the fact that his older twin was cutting him out!

Fortunately she was spared the need for a rejoinder by the dramatic entrance of her brother and Mary of Montlaine. They were announced, and all speech was halted as the assembled company turned to stare.

Chapter Fourteen

Edward Parks put down his fork and sat back in his chair to frown across his dining table at Montlaine.

"I tell you, Bret . . . something is afoot."

"But why do you say so?"

"I have it from your man Epps that the Echworths go to dinner at Penrod!"

"Impossible. Guss can't stand m'cousins, and well you know it. Besides, she would never extend an invitation with Mary in the house."

"So I thought. Nevertheless . . . they go tonight, and what is more, *Duncan is with them!*"

"Burn it! Never say he is here!"

"Well, as to that, I'm glad of it, as now we may proceed with our plans. He arrived some minutes after I took my leave of Sheila and went into town. On my return trip I met Epps in the field and he gave me word."

Montlaine pushed his plate away and leaned on his elbows. "I'm worried, Edward . . . Duncan coming just at this time . . . what with Lady Penrod having a houseful of guests . . ."

"You fear one of Lady Penrod's guests will give Mary away?"

He moved restlessly and finally stood up. "The only one who knows of Mary's presence in the Penrod household is Lady Vanessa."

"She has not given *you* away, Bret." He too got to his feet. "Why would she divulge Mary's presence?"

"Who knows what a woman will do?"

"I will agree with you there." Edward grinned and then grew more somber. "And come to think of it... she seemed rather taken with Orson."

"With Orson? I can't credit it! Why, he ain't in the petticoat line and wouldn't know how to turn a pretty compliment even for a beauty like Naughty Lady Ness!" scoffed the viscount.

"Nevertheless, he seemed to be doing just that the other night when we had dinner at Montlaine. Still... she said nothing about you when your name was mentioned, and frankly I think the woman means to keep your secret."

The viscount said nothing to this. Instead he pulled out a decanter of port from the glass cabinet near him and poured out two glasses. One of these he handed to his friend, the other he downed. "I'm off, Edward..."

"Ho there, my friend, not so fast. The hour wants but ten minutes to nine. It is far too early for you to make tracks. Best wait until all the revelers are safely tucked away."

The viscount of Montlaine fidgeted. He wanted to return to his cave. Why, he could not say, or would not. He only knew he wanted to ride his stallion and make for his cave, where there was a possibility, though a slight one, that Lady Vanessa Grey might attend him. Confound it! Ah, who was he trying to bamboozle? After his unpardonable behavior she would come to him no more. He should count himself lucky if she kept her promise not to give him away! He poured himself another glassful and under the disapproving eye of his friend once again downed its contents.

The time at Penrod did not drag by slowly as it did for the viscount at Edward Parks's establishment. Such was the entertainment. Lady Vanessa took a backseat to the proceedings, watching penetratingly the various reactions to Mary's entrance upon the scene.

Mrs. Echworth was moved to a convulsive display of feelings. Sheila's attitude could not be checked and flowed freely, while her brothers remained silent at first.

"You should be ashamed of yourself, cousin Mary!" ejaculated Sheila after the initial show of relief to find her well. "How can you have put Mother to so much grief and worry?"

"Indeed, Mary, it was most thoughtless of you," added Mrs. Echworth, putting a handkerchief to her eyes.

"I should think we might consider Mary's emotional state before we allow ourselves to run the girl through!" put in Duncan Echworth kindly. From the corner of his eye he watched for Vanessa's reaction to his show of gentleness.

"Agreed," put in Lady Penrod, suddenly taking command of the situation. "Mary has lost a brother under gravely frightening circumstances. I understand from the friends she has been with this last month that she was in an emotional and physical decline. I should think the last thing she needs now is chastisement."

"Do you mean that she wasn't here . . . with you?" demanded Sheila.

"Why, my dear . . . Mary has only just arrived at Penrod this very afternoon," lied Lady Penrod without a trace of guilt. More and more she was convinced that the Echworths meant Mary of Montlaine mischief.

"Where have you been then, Mary?" This from Mrs. Echworth.

Mary had not until this moment said a word. She was overcome to find the Echworths had already discarded their mourning clothes. Bitterly she retorted, "It doesn't matter. I am here now."

"How dare you speak to Mother in that tone!" put in Sheila.

"I think, Sheila, you take affront too easily," said Duncan, his gentle voice belying the severity of his glance. "Our cousin has suffered through an ordeal. We are thankful she has returned to us."

"Oh, but she hasn't," said Richard of Grey suddenly.

Duncan frowned. "What is that supposed to imply?"

"I am sorry, Mr. Echworth. I know you wish to have Mary safely under your guardianship, but it is Mary's wish to remain with Lady Penrod, and as it has also been her doctor's advice, we feel certain you will honor it," returned Richard adroitly.

"Nonsense. Mary will be much better once she has returned to her home."

"I won't go. Every thing at Montlaine will remind me of Bret, and I am just not ready to ... to ..." She turned dramatically and buried her face in Richard's coat, pulling at the lapels for emphasis of feeling.

"There, there ..." said Richard. In a whisper he demanded she release his lapels before she damaged them. Aloud he said, "You needn't go to Montlaine until you are ready. Isn't that right, Mr. Echworth?"

Clearly Mr. Duncan Echworth found himself nonplussed. To insist on her return to Montlaine in view of what they had in mind for Mary would appear suspicious in the extreme. And there was Lady Vanessa, saying little and perhaps reserving judgment. He wanted her good opinion, and perhaps in the end it would be best for Mary to remain at Penrod. Indeed, perhaps it would be to their advantage.

"Of course if Lady Penrod doesn't mind, Mary may stay here," returned Duncan carefully.

"What?" This from Sheila. "Duncan . . . the chit plays us for fools!"

"Do control yourself, Sheila. I am certain upon further reflection you will find yourself sadly out on this issue," whispered Orson from behind her shoulder. She turned to study him. She didn't know what her twin brothers had in mind. They had never let her in on their plans. But she hadn't been duped by their masquerade and had made some very accurate guesses as to the charade's purposes. She checked what next she wanted to say and left it to Duncan to command.

It was at this point that Toby entered and announced dinner. Lady Vanessa found herself led into the dining room by Duncan, who made an excellent attempt to turn her mind from the problem of Mary and concentrate her thoughts on himself. He was to all outward purposes a veritable charmer. A scamp, a delightful rogue, and had she not known better she would have been greatly diverted by his wit. However, she did know better, much better.

It was nearly midnight when the viscount of Montlaine arrived at his seaside habitat. He lit a candle, stuck it wearily into its holder on a flat rock near the opening of the cave and began untacking his horse. The stallion seemed cool enough to put away, and this he did before throwing off his cape and lounging back on his straw bed. He put his hands behind his head.

169

Would she come this eve? No. Why should she? Indeed, she had every reason not to.

Confound the woman! He was up on his feet again, moving restlessly. It was a sultry evening, and quickly he undid his cravat, removed his coat and his waistcoat, dropped them in a neat pile on his makeshift table. She had cut up his peace with her sparkling eyes and her mischievous smile. Why hadn't she given him away? The passing hours had given him time to reflect. He hadn't wanted to think about Vanessa, but thoughts do push themselves intrusively against the will. Furiously he relived their last meeting and its horrendous results. Nothing had turned out as he had planned, and fortune was surely proving itself a female and a hardened one at that!

Burn it! Why had he treated her so brutishly? What had come over him? And what in blazes did Edward mean by connecting Echworth's name to that of Lady Vanessa? Was there a courtship underfoot? It was at this moment that a sound caught his attention, and he spun round to find Lady Vanessa standing at the portal of his cave. There was no smile on her countenance, there was no pleasure in her gaze. She seemed cold, distant and businesslike. Still, he felt a wealth of feeling rush through his body. More than excitement, less than satisfaction, and useless to deny. Her expression however, angered him, and he made her a mock bow,

"Ah, so Lady Vanessa once again seeks the forbidden?"

She stamped her foot. "You are despicable!" A moment's hesitation. She should leave. He wasn't worth the effort.

He saw it in her expression and moved with alacrity. His hand reached for and acquired her arm beneath the cape, and gently he stayed her. "Forgive me."

She eyed him suspiciously but relented. "Very well." She took a step into the cave and pulled out of his touch. It was too confusing being so very near to him. She undid the tiestrings of her cloak and draped it over a group of rocks. She was clothed once again in shirt and breeches. He said nothing to this, but she was on the defensive. "Let us first understand one thing, my lord. I don't give a jot for your good opinions. I came here because there is much that has happened today that will affect your future. I don't owe you this visit, I don't owe you my help or my consideration, but you will get it anyway, because I think your sister is a jewel worth saving! I don't intend to let my dislike of you alter my decision to assist your sister to clear the name of Montlaine!"

He inclined his head. "I suppose I must thank you."

She discovered that his hair fell forward in most provocative waves, that in those waves were lights of iridescent hue. She brushed such nonsense from her mind. He was rude and arrogant.

"No, you must not do such a thing. It would not be in keeping with your character!"

He smiled naturally at last. "My lady's tongue is as sharp as her bright eyes, and pierces all."

"Shall we banter all the night away, or shall I tell you why I am here?"

He laughed, shortly. "Indeed, sweetheart, do tell me why you are here."

She put up her chin at the use of the endearment, decided to let it go and proceeded, "It is rather complicated...and I am not certain just how I should begin..."

"Begin at the heart of it. We wouldn't want you to risk wasting your valuable time sparing my feelings," he said dryly.

She eyed him fulminatingly. "*Wretch!* Deuce take you, rogue! As it happens, what I am risking is involving myself in yet another scrape society will no doubt add to my list of deplorable doings!"

His smile softened, and his hand reached out and found her chin. "Ah no, my beauty, only the vulgar would call this last entanglement a scrape. The learned are more apt to describe it as a dilemma."

She moved away from him. "Shall I tell you what has transpired today or not? I have been here longer than I care to be, and not one word of my purpose has yet been said," declared the lady on an exasperated note.

Something mellowed within him. Perhaps because of the sudden edge of desperation in her tone. Perhaps because he made the momentous error of looking across at her to find her eyes.

"Do sit with me, my lady, and do ... tell me all."

She searched his face, and finding there an honest welcome she allowed him to lead her to the straw bedding, where she sat and tucked in her legs beneath her. He laughed and stretched out beside her. She pulled a face at him, and he gestured with his hand. "Now, my lady, what has brought you out to me at this hour?"

"Oh dear, I fear you will not be pleased with everything ... but never mind. I shall start by telling you about Bess Widdons."

"Go on, what about the chit?"

"For one thing, she was a member of the coven ..."

"What coven? You mean ... there really was a coven?" He was startled.

"Why yes, of course. All that couldn't be made up just to blame you. You didn't think the vicar was actually lying about it?" She was surprised.

"I just wasn't sure there was an actual coven of twelve girls. It seems absurd!"

"Well, absurd or not, there was a coven of twelve girls controlled by a male member calling himself the master. Evidently he had the girls convinced that he was lord of Montlaine..."

"Swine!"

"Yes. However, he made his first major error when he seduced poor Melony Fry. I mean...he allowed her to see who he was...didn't he?" She proceeded to answer her own question. "Well, he must have, because they became very intimate and Melony found herself with child. Melony demanded marriage. He refused. She threatened to destroy his plans, perhaps expose him. Melony was poisoned."

"Yes...yes, I quite see...but it doesn't bring us any closer to the truth. If Melony was the only person who knew this creature's identity..."

"He is no animal, but a very cunning, very wicked man," corrected Vanessa gravely. "And I have a strong suspicion that Bess knows more than she is saying but is afraid to tell me."

"Afraid?"

"Well...he did kill Melony, didn't he?"

"But she could be taken into protective custody."

"Precisely so, and I mean to point it out to her when next I speak to the girl. I wanted some time to go by after our talk this morning. I wanted her to think about it." She gave him a long look. "And speaking about protective custody brings me to Mary."

"What about Mary?" he asked sharply.

"You needn't look as though you would like to eat me!" she charged.

He grinned. "Oh, but I would...I most certainly would."

She blushed furiously. "Stop it! Now, to be serious, my lord, Mary has decided to come out into the open."

"What?" He came up off his elbow and sat up straight

173

as he took her shoulders in his firm grasp. "Was this *your* doing?"

She moved her features. "As to that...I didn't discourage her..."

"My God! What can you have had in your mind? You will go back with but one purpose, to keep my sister out of the Echworths' reach. Is that understood, Lady Vanessa?"

"Oh, don't be a fool. Did you think I would actually allow Mary to return to Montlaine?"

He breathed a sigh of relief. "What, then?"

"She remains at Penrod...but has tonight met with the Echworths at dinner under Lady Penrod's chaperonage."

"Devil you say!" He was furious. "Do you realize what you have done?"

"More important, Mary realizes fully what she has done. We mean to keep her at Penrod, where she is recovering from the shock of your death. Both my brother and my cousin are pledged to protect her. You need have no fear, and there is every good chance this is where our master devil might slip up."

He did not say anything to this but turned away from her. She felt his hands slip away and for a moment wished he were holding her still in his grip. "My lord...there is more."

"Devil a bit...there couldn't be." He groaned.

"Duncan has returned."

"No doubt to pick up his title and estates. Well, he shan't have them just yet." He looked at her penetratingly. "I am told his brother would have you...if he could."

She gave him an arch look. "Well, well, you do manage to stay informed." She smiled amiably. "As a matter of fact, yesterday I would have agreed with you. Orson did seem very interested in me. Tonight was an

174

entirely different scene. It was not Orson who sought my favor but Duncan."

"Well, that at least is in Duncan's nature ... to flirt with a beautiful woman. It was not Orson's habit to seek out that sort of occupation."

"Hmmm. It is all very odd, though ... they are so alike, and yet ..."

"They are twins," he remarked, cutting her off. "There is nothing remarkable in their looking like one another."

"You don't understand. Duncan seems more Orson than Orson does."

"You are quite correct, of course. I don't understand in the least."

"I really don't know how to explain this ... but every individual gives off something of himself ... herself ... an undefinable air. Sometimes it misleads us into false conclusions about the individual's character. Orson is now different. His air, if you will, has a different scent, a different color ... while Duncan is totally familiar."

"This perhaps because Orson lost interest and Duncan picked it up?" he returned dryly.

"Perhaps ... but I don't think so."

"Then what is the answer?" He asked the question, but he wasn't really taking this issue seriously.

"I don't know. I am just being silly, perhaps."

"Do let us return then to the subject of Mary. You said you mean to have her protected by your brother and cousin ... watched over by them?"

"Yes, I think it will serve."

"Really?" His face was drawn in sarcasm. "Only do but observe how well they look after you!"

"That was not a nice remark. Mary will not want to elude them ... and they are not in fear for my life," she returned angrily.

"Perhaps not your life, but your reputation. No doubt

175

your brother was sent to Cornwall with you to keep you in charge?"

"That is an idiotish thing to suppose!" snapped the lady, incensed. "My brother is my junior. He was not sent to Cornwall to keep an eye on me but to bear me company. Besides, he had fallen out of favor with my papa for his part in my . . . little adventure."

Momentarily diverted, the viscount's mobile brow moved. "Just what had you done to land yourself in Cornwall?"

"It was the veriest nothing."

"Oh, that bad, eh?"

"Not at all. My horse was challenged . . . the argument got out of hand and it ended by my telling a slightly foxed gentleman (who has long been a thorn in my side) that not only could my mare beat his gelding, but that she could do it with me on her back. So, we ran the race before my parents were due to arrive in Brighton. However, as there were wagers placed and won, word reached London and my parents' ears. Alas, Naughty Lady Ness had once again landed herself in another scrape. My parents came down with a strong lecture over my head, issued much the same to my brother for having been on the spot and not doing anything to stop me . . . as though he could, but never mind. Cornwall is not so very bad."

"But . . . did you win?"

She laughed. "I did, of course. I knew that I should. His bay is strong enough in the works, but his lordship was ever ham-handed, never could get the most out of his animals!"

He was chuckling low in his throat. "And this cousin of yours . . ." He watched her face searchingly. "He came along to bear *you* company, no doubt?"

"Randall? He came under protest and at the insistence of my brother. Rick would have it that my mess was all due to his bringing my mare's name into the argument with Lord Walton. Oh, but it doesn't signify..."

"Then Randall...your cousin...has no bent in your direction?"

"What? You think Randall is one of my admirers?" Ness laughed. "I doubt that he even thinks me a girl. We quite grew up in each other's way, you see..."

The viscount seemed pleased with this, but he took her hand and as he stood he helped her to her feet. The fresh scent of her filled his senses, and for a sudden heady moment he thought he was floating in a bed of wildflowers. Obtrusively the thought also attended him that Duncan had been this close to her. It rankled. His hands found her waist and drew her nearer still.

"How far, Vanessa...just how far did you encourage Duncan Echworth?"

She searched his eyes, such black firelit eyes. He was so like quicksilver, and she knew a sudden need to comfort him. "Not nearly as far as I encourage you." It was out before she realized it. The tone had been teasing enough, but the words had come from her heart.

His arms clasped her tightly, and his head bent to her own reaching arms. Her mouth was sweet to his taste, and his kiss wavered on the edge of tenderness and passion until he pushed her away from him with a force. "Ah, Vanessa...your play is too dangerous, even for me." He sighed sadly. "You had better go."

She was deflated. Her brows drew together, and her gray eyes darkened with her disappointment. Those were not the words she would hear. There was nothing she could say. Why was this man forever finding fault with her? Why was he forever rejecting her in one manner or another? She moved to the mouth of the cave where she had tethered her mare and turning back she said quietly, "You judge me still by rumor. 'Tis odd, for you would have yourself judged by truth. You, my lord, are the one who is playing... and not fairly!" With that she hoisted herself into her saddle and before he could think to reply took to the beach.

Chapter Fifteen

Richard of Grey flung off his superfine after which followed his waistcoat and cravat. He gave them a good swift kick across the room and stood to gaze at himself in his looking glass. "You are naught but a moonling!" he told his reflection disgustedly. "You never saw her for what she was...did you? Fool!"

This because he had discovered that his lovely Sheila was something of a grasping miss with little or no sensibility. The fact that her character had been disguised by her looks bothered his sense of seemliness in himself. He wasn't sure if Sheila had been a part of the underhandedness that had taken place at Montlaine, but it surely had been obvious that she wanted Mary under their own management. Why? She showed no great love for the girl.

There too he was moved to deeper, graver suspicions of both Orson and Duncan Echworth. Richard of Grey had watched these two brothers closely during the evening. There were mysterious looks passed between the two after Mary's appearance on the scene. He had listened to their conversation, had observed their expressions when they were silent and had come away with an uncomfortable feeling. Thank God Mary was safely tucked away in her tower room above. No one could get the child there!

A knock sounded on his door, and with a brow upraised he went to it and pulled it wide.

"Mary!" he exclaimed with surprise and gentle disapproval.

"May I come in, Richard? I couldn't sleep . . ."

He frowned. "Well . . . only a moment . . . and leave the door open, girl . . . that's it. Now . . . sit down and tell me what's fretting you."

"A few things . . . and I am sorry to bother you . . . I wouldn't have, but I am a little worried. You see, I wanted to talk . . . so I went to your sister's room . . . and Richard . . ." She lowered her voice. "She isn't there."

"Isn't she, by Jove?"

"No, and though it has me worried, I thought I had better come to you rather than to Lady Penrod."

"Lady Penrod? Good God, what a thing to suggest! Dashed glad you came to me." He sighed. "No doubt Ness is on one of her junkets. Restless sort, is Ness . . . never thinks twice but there she is off on her mare. Don't like her going out at this hour, but daresay she was in a rare taking after this evening's doings. Likes a good run when her mind's in a pucker."

"Yes, but . . . do you think she will be all right?"

"Ness? Never knew a girl like her." He gave a little chuckle. "My father would go off in an apoplexy if he knew she was careening over the moors at this hour, but she'll do. What she wants is a man to tame her. Never met one that was her match . . ." he mused.

Mary's eyes went distant. "I have."

"You don't say . . . who, by Jove?"

"My late brother..."

His voice softened. "Now, Mary... don't be running into the past, you're bound to stumble that route."

"Yes, I know..."

"Very well then, Mary, just why are you here?"

"I suppose I am just a bit frightened..."

He went to her and put a comforting arm around her shoulders, noting that she was trembling. "Here, have you no confidence in me, Mary?"

"That isn't it... oh, Richard, I didn't expect Duncan to be home. He... he means me harm... I sense it... felt it when he looked at me tonight... and Richard... he is all too interested in Vanessa."

"Ha... Vanessa doesn't give two hoots for that park-sauntering knave!"

"No? She did seem to get on with him."

"Did she? Well, no one can ever tell what is Ness's mind, but don't you worry. Now, let me take you upstairs..."

"You will make certain Vanessa gets in safely?"

"That I will, child. But come on... as young as you are you still shouldn't be in my room."

She pulled a face. he let go a laugh and took her hand and led her out of his chambers. A few moments later he saw her neatly, happily put away in her own quarters, and he descended the stairs to await his sister's arrival.

Duncan Echworth saw his family within the doors of Montlaine, whereupon he turned on his heel and returned to the stables for a horse. A passing of moments saw him once again on Penrod land.

Duncan Echworth was a man of strong instincts, and his instincts told him to return to Penrod that night. He had no idea why he should or what he would gain, but he had learned to profit too often from his sixth sense to ignore it now.

He took to horse and arrived on Penrod land some ten minutes later just in time to see the candlelight at the tower room move as Mary said goodnight and closed the door to Richard. Intrigued, he inched his horse into a better position, where he remained, and while he watched Mary paced. Who was it in the tower room? he wondered, and then had his question answered as Mary went to stand with her candle by the open window. Mary! Locked up out of reach in the tower? He smiled to himself. What then? Was she under guard? Did Lady Penrod suspect mischief in the air? Interesting. He would have to move carefully. It would present a difficulty. However, he would discover Mary's daily routine and choose the moment that suited his purposes.

Thus determined he turned his horse and left the grounds via the park. As he turned onto the road the sound of an approaching rider came to his ears. Quickly he pulled his horse up and backed him into the shadows.

Vanessa had attained the peak of the slope before she realized she had forgotten her cloak in the viscount's cave. She decided against returning for it, as she did not want another encounter with him this night. She had to think. He was blasting her logic, cutting up her peace, teaching her how very little she knew about the art of dalliance, an art she had thought herself not quite green at. No, she wasn't about to go back this night. So it was she rode across the moors with her auburn hair streaming down her back. The white linen shirt she wore flapped with the wind, and in the haze of the partial moonlight one could catch glimpses of her slim womanly figure as she paced her horse for home.

Vanessa never saw the shape of a man astride a horse in the dark shadows. She never sensed his excitement as she rode by. Duncan Echworth looked hard on her face as she left the road and took the private drive to the Penrod stables, and for a long time afterward he sat in puzzlement. What was she up to? Where had she been? Who had been with her?

Richard of Grey sat upon his sister's bed and waited. This was really too much! It was one thing if she chose to take a quick airing about the park grounds. But this...this was beyond everything, and damn, what would his father say? Thunder and turf! He knew just what his father would say.

Vanessa opened her door and tiptoed into her room quietly. There she breathed a sigh and was scouting with her hand for her branch of candles and the tinderbox when a dark shadowy figure moved toward her.

She put a hand to her throat and gasped, "Who is it?"

"Well you should ask!" returned her brother, handing her the tinderbox, "Now...bring the candles and let's have a talk, Ness."

She did this in silence, collecting her thoughts, before coming around to face him. "Well, Richard, I never thought you would take to spying on me," she said tartly.

"Don't be a ninny!" returned her brother. "Little Mary went to your room after we had all retired, and when she found you missing she came to me."

"And now I suppose you want an explanation."

"Famous! You have a knack of turning things around so that I begin to feel foolish. Anyone would

183

think by your attitude you had been doing naught but taking a stroll about the house in the light of day! Confound it, Ness! It's nearly one-thirty in the morning...you are in breeches...no hooded cloak...and no shame!"

"Shame? And why, Richard, should I feel any shame?" Her chin was well into the air.

"Because...though you may not like it...females just don't go about unescorted at night, especially at this hour! Ness, it just isn't the thing! Lord...what do you think Father would think?"

She looked a little troubled. "Father needn't know about it."

"If you persist in going out at this hour, I will have no choice but to advise him of your behavior," he said gravely.

"Richard! You wouldn't! Of all the traitorous...why, did I tell Papa the time you took the raft down the Avon and ditched yourself? No, I did not...I rescued you at some cost to myself. Did I tell Papa the time you and Randy and a set of your friends got foxed and landed yourselves in the basket up at Cambridge? No, I did not, I bailed you out with nary a word to our parents! Why, did I tell..."

"Stop! That ain't the point, Ness...and I won't like having to do you such a turn, but dash it, girl, this could have its consequences, and I fear it is my duty as your brother, even though I am your junior, to take measures to protect you!"

"Never mind. I don't think I shall be scampering about the countryside at the objectionable hour any more, so you needn't concern yourself with me."

"Won't you? Why?" Apparently this announcement did little to alleviate his fears.

She feigned amusement. "Now, look at you, darling. You don't want me riding out in the wee hours...and now you want to know why I have agreed not to."

"Don't play games, Ness. Where have you been going and why won't you be going any more? I can't believe it's because of our little talk just now ... or my threat."

"Well, it isn't because of your threat, for I don't care for such paltry things! Threaten me indeed! But I shall tell you what if you will stop being disagreeable."

"Then tell me."

"It is a confidence, Richard. I must have your word as a gentleman."

"You have it."

"Well then, I have been going to see Mary's brother ... to report to him what has been happening here and at Montlaine."

"The girl has gone mad," exclaimed Richard to no one in particular.

"Don't be a noddy. The viscount of Montlaine is alive," she said in a low voice. "The fall into the ocean did not kill him. He is alive and innocent and in need of help." —

"Mary ... Mary thinks he is dead."

"I know, poor child."

"But that is outrageous. The girl has been in deep mourning for him."

"It was necessary to keep the truth from her. Mary has to be protected. What do you think she would do if she knew he were alive?"

"Go to him, of course."

"Exactly."

"Yes, I quite see ... but Ness, what is to be done?"

"I don't know, though I can't help feeling Bess Widdons has more to tell. It is my belief that I could flush it out of her if Mary were to come with me."

"Mary ... oh no. That is a sight too dangerous. How am I to protect the girl if she is running about the moors with you?"

"But Richard, it would serve..."

"No it won't, for I don't mean to allow it!" he returned firmly.

"Oh, Richard..."

"Mind now. Mary stays within our grounds here, and you don't go riding Shadow at wild hours of the night. That is my final word." He waited for her answer, and when he received only her silence he urged, "Agreed?"

"Did you give me any choice?"

"Well then, it is settled. Goodnight, Ness, and don't take it so. You may be miffed with me now, but someday you will thank me, see if you don't." With which he left his sister on her own and returned to his room feeling quite accomplished. Had he realized that she still had not given him an inch on anything he would have felt very much worse about their little talk!

Spears of sunlight shot through the overhanging branches onto the main pike. A sweet breeze shifted the green leaves, bent their stalks and brought the scent of wildflowers to all who would enjoy. Bess Widdons left the dales and took the road, but she was insensible to the loveliness of the summer's day. She guided her old and gentle roan over the badly rutted shale and dirt road toward Penrod Tower. The note she had received from Lady Vanessa that very morning was tucked into her reticule, which hung at her wrist. She felt the sun on her face and pulled her straw bonnet lower over her forehead. She didn't want to be here. She didn't want to meet Lady Vanessa this morning, but she had been given little choice.

She had read Vanessa's note with great misgiving and a strong conviction that only trouble would come of this meeting. Vanessa had bade her come and in such a way she dared not refuse. She had no wish for

Lady Vanessa to visit her at her parents' home. She had no wish for Lady Vanessa to go with what she knew to her parents. Better to come to her... pacify her... keep her away from Widdons's mill.

The Tower with its mellowed gray battlement reposed at the top of the hill flanking the road. A barrage of evergreen and rhododendrons no longer in bloom moved into harmony with the wide black iron gate displaying the Penrod coat of arms. Then she caught sight of Vanessa, and Bess's heart skipped nervously within her breast.

Vanessa's simple day gown of dotted yellow muslin moved elegantly with the sway of her walk. She looked a veritable girl with her auburn curls caught at the nape of her neck with a yellow ribbon. The green lawns of Penrod stretched out at her back, and Bess found herself relaxing, even smiling a greeting as she jumped off her roan and guided him through the thicket to join Vanessa.

"Hallo!" cried Vanessa merrily enough.

Bess lifted her hand in response, but the smile died on her face when she saw tripping lightly behind Lady Vanessa a petite girl in white whom she recognized as Mary of Montlaine.

Lady Vanessa extended her hand. "Bess... please do calm yourself. You look frightened to death. No one here means you any harm." She pressed her forward, taking the roan's reins. "Look... we've brought a halter and line. We can tether your horse here and take a bit of a walk together... away from the house, if you like."

Bess nodded but stood back, her face a measure of consternation as she avoided Mary's dark searching eye. "I... I don't really understand... what you want..." she offered as Lady Vanessa finished with the roan and linked her arm.

"Don't you, Bess? I think you do, and I can understand why you are hesitant about lending us your help."

Bess turned to Mary. "Please, my lady... I am so sorry about your brother..."

"I believe you are, but that doesn't help. Being sorry is sometimes just not enough," said Mary gravely.

Bess found that she could say nothing to this and turned away in some confusion. Vanessa interceded gently, "You see, Bess... *Duncan is home.*"

"Is he?" returned the girl warily. "Why should that make a difference?"

"He is here to settle the estate and to take Mary to Montlaine," said Vanessa on a quiet note.

"Oh No! No ... you mustn't let him do that!"

"Do what, Bess?" asked Vanessa, carefully restraining her excitement. So then Bess did know more than she had let on!

"Lady Mary mustn't go with him to Montlaine ... she mustn't!" cried the girl distractedly.

"But Bess ... he is my cousin," said Mary. Her dark eyes met Vanessa's and then returned to look imploringly into Bess's. "Is there something you know about him ... that you want to tell me?"

"No! No ... I know nothing. Please ... let me go ... I have to return home."

"Bess ... don't you like Duncan Echworth?" This from Vanessa.

"I ... I ... oh, please, I don't know him ... how should I like or dislike him?" returned Bess, on the edge of hysteria.

Vanessa took her by the shoulders firmly, and her voice was both imperious and authoritive. "Bess Widdons, get yourself together and tell us what you are hiding!"

Duncan Echworth lifted his gray top hat and ran a hand over his pale-gold hair before resetting the hat once again on his head and urging his horse forward. However, as he rounded the bend he saw a girl astride a roan. She was a lanky girl not worth his attention was his first reaction to this vision. However, the girl's movements intrigued his notice, for what did she do but slip off her roan and move into the thickets bordering the Penrod estate.

He was himself on his way to Penrod Tower to court the fair Vanessa, and so he urged his horse forward quietly until he caught sight of first Vanessa and then Mary greeting the girl and proceeding to walk along a path through the woods.

A moment later his horse was secured and he was on foot at a discreet but convenient distance from the party. There was something about the tall thin girl that seemed somehow familiar, but then he was always finding something familiar between one wench and another. Bess? Vanessa had called her Bess, and then a flood of memory served to drain the blood from his cheek.

She would have to be silenced, and immediately! Why hadn't he realized that Melony might have confided in her? Damn, but this had been a mistake. His pistol he had not brought with him, but there was something he had always.... He rushed to his horse, disengaged the weapon from its resting place at the saddle's cantle and led his horse behind him. He would have to wait for the right moment and be quick about getting away!

"I don't know what you want me to say! I won't...I can't...now leave me alone...please..." begged Bess.

"Oh, Bess...how can you be so insensitive? Is it because you are afraid...afraid he might do you harm?

189

How can he if you would but give us his name? We would see to it that he could never harm you," asseverated Vanessa.

"What I could tell you wouldn't be enough! Don't you see . . . he would still go free . . . and he might then want revenge. No, you can't make me say anything."

"Bess, I don't believe you mean that," cried Mary on a note of horror. "What can you be thinking? He has already killed your friend . . . caused the death of my brother. Bess, he is a murderer! *You are protecting a murderer!*" She picked up the girl's trembling hand and squeezed it for emphasis. "If you think you know who this man is, you must tell us."

"I . . . oh, heaven forgive me, Lady Mary . . . I am so frightened," returned Bess on a sob.

A nearly imperceptible movement in the brush some distance at Vanessa's back sent a chill up her spine. She turned over her shoulder but could see nothing to warrant any undue concern. Then quite suddenly her eyes were fascinated with the multi-beamed illumination the sun will produce when one of its rays meets and bounces off a sleek metal object. Vanessa's mind worked like the insides of a well-running clock, taking in each piece of information, sorting, putting it together and all within the fraction of a second giving her an answer. She let go a short cry of terror, and rushed at Mary, pushing her down in one movement. Mary's foot came up as she went tumbling to the ground, and it caught Bess's knee sharply. Bess cried out in pain and bent to cup her knee with her hand. The blade had been released at the point of Vanessa's scream. It sped furiously through the air and planted itself with a resonant thud in the bark of a wide oak tree just behind Bess Widdons's right shoulder!

Vanessa's heart was pumping wildly, for her body had gone stiff. She had to move. She had to do something. Breathe, she told herself, for goodness sake ...*breathe!* At last, she found her voice, managed to move her limbs. "Stay here!" she commanded and without further pause took off into the woods. Some distance ahead of her she could hear the crashing of twigs beneath a heavy boot. She could hear a horse snort as its master mounted and cropped him sharply. She could hear the hooves, feel their pounding on the earth as the ground vibrated. She rounded the bend in the thicket and came out onto the road. There she was greeted by a cloud of dust as the rider made good his escape.

She stood a moment and then turned to rush back to the girls. Vanessa returned to the scene in time to stop Mary from landing Bess a blow, for thus she stood with her small fist clenched.

"Mary...calm yourself," urged Vanessa as she helped Mary brush the dirt off her white muslin.

"Then tell this ninnyhammer to keep her mummer shut, for if she don't stop wailing at me, Vanessa, I shall box her ears!"

"Yes, really, Bess...you are quite safe and there is nothing to be crying over *now*."

"But...that...that is a knife!" whimpered Bess.

"So it is, chit, and it was meant for me, so you can stop your blubbering!" thundered Mary irately.

Vanessa might have found all this amusing had she not already been sobered once again by looking at the knife lodged in the tree. "Actually...I think you are out there, Mary," said Vanessa thoughtfully. "*You* were not standing in line with this tree...Bess was. In fact, had Bess not bent at that precise moment, the knife would have caught her...directly in her chest."

Bess heard this, let go a moan and sank immediately to the ground. "Oh, dear," sighed Vanessa. "Bess ...Bess..." She bent to rouse the girl and was greeted

191

by the sound of a male voice at her back.

"Eh? Whats all this?" demanded Richard of Grey, crossing the lawn and entering in upon the cozy scene.

"Richard!" cried Mary happily. "You are here. Oh, Richard, such things have been happening! Someone has tried to kill me..."

"What?" ejaculated Richard.

"Don't interrupt!" returned Mary. "For Vanessa says he didn't try to kill me after all, it was Bess he wanted to kill."

"Bess? Bess?" Richard frowned, lighting on the lanky girl huddled in his sister's arms. Vanessa had finally managed to rouse her into consciousness.

"Yes, Bess Widdons...only you can see she isn't dead at all, so everything has worked out right and tight," declared Mary merrily.

"But...did you see..." He then discovered the marble-handled blade wedged into the tree's bark. "By Jove, look at this!" With which he dislodged it and let out a low whistle. "Our man meant business. But Vanessa, how do you know this wasn't meant for Mary?"

"I don't have time now, Richard. Take the girls up to the house. See to it that Bess is made comfortable and that a note is sent to her parents, for I don't mean to let her leave Penrod!" She started to move off in the direction of the stables.

"But...but...Ness...hold a moment...Ness?" cried Richard desperately. "Where are you going?"

"I am taking a drive to Montlaine! Don't worry... I am in no danger, Richard, but both your charges are. See to their safety!"

This hit Richard very severely. He let go a long audible sigh and turned to find Mary scolding Bess once again for being a dreadfully hysterical female. He allowed himself a moment to raise his eyes heavenward before attempting to take the situation in hand.

Chapter Sixteen

Edward Parks gave his horse over to Epps, and though there was a proper smile on his lips, his eyes were hard and stern. "Lord, but he did come riding in! I tried to catch up to him and never saw ought but the trial of dust he left behind. What's to do, Epps?"

The small wiry groom rubbed his chin and shook his head.

"I be stalled raight well Mr. Parks. He came in like the divil 'imself was a-thumping his tail. He gave m'lad some whisker aboot the roan getting away wit 'im."

"He never did? Why, that roan could no more get away ... well, well. I just think I'll go up to the house and see what tale he has to tell *me*. Where are the ladies?"

"Wit' Mr. Orson ... went shopping, they said."

"All right then, let's see what Mr. Duncan has to say to me."

"That oughta discumbuddle 'im reel proper, for I'll wager a monkey he's been up to prime bobbery this morn!"

Lady Vanessa drove her unicorn curricle at a spanking pace, hoping the blood they had hitched to the precarious piece of driving equipment was as fit as he looked, for she was driving him hard. She took her corners sharply and grimaced to think what her papa would say if he could see her riding unattended, without hat or gloves and at such an indecorous speed.

Finally she was on the long winding lane to Montlaine, and it suddenly hit her how very odd her remarkable arrival would appear. She slowed her horse and bit her lip as she searched her head for a ready excuse. With any luck Mrs. Echworth and Sheila would simply consider her behavior hoydenish and leave it at that. But Duncan, Orson ... would they be fooled?

As she pondered this she came within view of the stables and noticed a young boy walking a lathered roan. Past him to the stable doors she saw Epps waving off Edward Parks. Parks? Was that poor sweating animal Parks's steed? Had it been Parks in the woods at Penrod? No ... oh no ... not the viscount's friend? But why? What was his purpose? For Sheila? Was he doing it for Sheila?

She reined in and applied the brake with the sturdy stick at her side. Epps ambled over to her, and she wasn't surprised at all by his disapproving gleam. "M'lady ... 'ere now ... careful cooming down." He reached out his hand and she took hold of his wrist as she jumped nimbly down from her heights and smoothed out her gown.

She caught her breath and said sweetly, "Thank you ... Epps ... isn't it?"

"Aye ... and whot's this?" he said, running his hand down the horse's neck between its fores. "He be 'ot, m'lady ... I'll 'ave 'im walked fer ye."

"Thank you. I hope he won't be too much trouble. I

194

see one of your boys is already walking down Mr. Parks's horse," she said idly.

"Eh? Och now . . . that ain't Mr. Parks's horse." But he volunteered nothing more.

"Well then, I'll just go up to the house. Thank you, Epps."

More disheveled than usual, Duncan composed himself to face Edward Parks. They were alone in the library as Duncan poured two glasses of sherry and made the man reasonably welcome.

"So then, Mr. Parks, Orson tells me you have made an interesting proposition to us."

"Proposition? That is not what I would call it," returned Parks casually. He took the proffered glass and and sat down to observe his host's reaction.

"No? Perhaps then I am mistaken. What is it you would call . . . your offer?"

"Not an offer at all, Duncan. It was something of an ultimatum," returned Parks quietly.

"Indeed?" Duncan's brow went up. It had been he and not Orson who had conducted that last meeting with Edward Parks, and as he remembered no threat had been issued. What had changed?

"I don't see that you have anything viable, Parks."

"Don't you? You don't give Sheila enough credit. There is a great deal she wants, and I want it for her."

"Ah, but you see, I intend to take care of Sheila . . . and as the matter of Mary's future is now in *my* hands . . ."

"Mary's future?"

"Yes, that's right, you will not have heard yet. Mary is at Penrod. She did us the honor of presenting herself to us last night, and we expect she will soon come home. What then can *you* offer?"

"A threat, good sir. A very ominous threat, for you

see I know who it was who led the cult meetings. Sheila discovered you very early in your game ... or rather Orson ... for you were in London, weren't you?" It was said on a sneer.

Duncan laughed shortly. "Sheila seems to think she knows a great deal. But Parks, knowing and proving, as your legal mind must comprehend, are two different matters!"

"Together, Sheila and I could prove a great deal. She is your sister, but would if crossed do you harm ... and more important, she has the means to accomplish it."

"Does she? May I inquire what exactly Sheila has?"

Parks did not have to search for an answer, because they were interrupted by the announcement of Lady Vanessa's presence. The library door was held back by the butler, and there Vanessa stood, slightly wind-blown but alluringly lovely in her yellow gown and with her bright gray eyes. Her brow arched as she inclined her head and stepped forward to Duncan's hearty welcome.

He crossed the room in quick easy strides and took up her hand, bending to its perfect whiteness with charming grace. "My lovely Lady Vanessa. I have been thinking about you all the morning, and now here you are. Is it possible you read my mind?"

"Wretch!" She smiled. "Do you suggest that I would come running to your bidding?"

"A fond hope, but it seems I am out." He chuckled. "Do sit, I will ring for some lemonade."

Edward Parks moved to her side as Duncan went to the bellrope. His voice was low, conspiratorial. "All is well at Penrod, I hope?"

She smiled at him. "Odd, sir, that you should say that, for no, I regret to inform you that all is far from being well up at the Tower!"

Duncan turned, and as he retraced his steps to her side he was frowning.

"What can you mean? Mary? Is Mary safe?"

"Rest easy, sir, your cousin is quite safe...though we are not sure she was meant to be."

"What are you saying, Lady Vanessa?" asked Parks sharply.

"It is rather complicated. You see...this young woman, Bess Widdons by name, came to see Mary this morning. Word does get out quickly, and when Miss Widdons realized that Mary was at Penrod she sent a note around asking to meet with her outside the house. I naturally accompanied Mary..."

"Naturally? How so?" This from Duncan, and it was apparent he was restraining his temper.

"Ah, my brother has some silly notion that Mary might yet be in danger."

"Really? From whom?" Again from Duncan, and this time he feigned insult.

"Why...from the townsfolk, of course," she put in innocently. "But never mind...what I am here to tell you is that someone *did* attempt to kill Mary this morning, though he took very bad aim and nearly caught Bess Widdons in the attempt!" She wasn't about to let him know they believed Bess had been the target.

"My God!" breathed Parks.

"Precisely," agreed Vanessa nodding her head.

"This has gone beyond the limits!" shouted Duncan.

"What shall we do?" asked Vanessa.

"Where is Mary now?" asked Duncan.

"Within the Tower of course. My brother has her safely within his watch."

"And Miss Widdons?" further inquired Duncan.

"We are keeping her at the Tower as well."

"Really? I don't see the sense in that," returned Dun-

197

can. "You said the attempt was made against Mary ... not Miss Widdons."

"Yes. However, my brother feels that the girl is too prostrate from the ordeal to return home just yet."

"This is all very distressing," put in Parks. "It is a wonder that the scoundrel missed his target."

"It was the veriest chance that he did. Something in the wood frightened me you see ..."

"You saw Mary's assailant?" Duncan appeared white with rage.

"No, only a movement in the woods ... but it frightened me and I pushed Mary in my haste to run away. She fell down, and like dominoes, Bess went down a bit as well."

"And so he got away," added Parks. "I don't suppose any of you thought to try to catch a glimpse of the fellow?"

"As a matter of fact I did ... but unfortunately he was riding hard and kicking up a devil of a storm at his back. I couldn't catch a good look at either the rider or the horse."

"It could have been a woman?" suggested Duncan.

"No, I don't think so," said Vanessa.

"A woman *could* fire a gun as well as a man?" suggested Parks. "Though personally, I don't believe it." He looked directly at Duncan.

"Oh, but it wasn't a gun that was fired," said Vanessa, thinking that it was too bad Parks had opened his mouth here. She had been hoping to trap Duncan into mentioning the knife. She had been so careful to avoid mentioning the weapon herself.

"What then?" This from Parks.

"A knife. A rather unusual one with a marble handle," returned Vanessa, watching Duncan's face.

"Pardon me, my lady. Would you mind terribly if I left you with Duncan? I should like to ride over to

Penrod immediately and inspect the weapon."

"Yes, do that ... my brother has it in charge."

He made her his bow and was off. Duncan stood a few moments before giving Vanessa his full attention. He had acted too quickly this morning. He had not thought the thing out. Bess Widdons was turning out to be a costly mistake. His sister too would have to be dealt with, and there was Parks. But for now, here was Vanessa ... and he had a few unanswered questions that needed to be put to the lady.

He took her hand and smiled. "Come, Vanessa ... walk with me. I have a great deal to talk to you about, and this is not the mood I would set."

She hesitated and then allowed him to pull her to her feet. "That, I think, would be lovely. I do so enjoy a walk in the fresh air when I am all to pieces."

"And are you all to pieces now? I don't think so. No, I think you are the sort that always knows just what to do."

"Am I? What makes you say so? For I must point out to you, sir, that you hardly know me."

That was right. As Duncan, he had first met her only last night. "Intuition. I know it is a gift attributed to women, but I have often found that impressions of another's character are fostered by a sixth sense that I suspect both men and women of high intellect own to some degree."

She laughed and allowed him to lead her through the garden doors. They passed neat flower beds, rows of orchards in full bloom, and came upon a man-made pond resting between two large green willow trees. Here he led her to a bench, where he seated her gently before taking up a position beside her. They had been passing the time with mundane and idle chatter, and it was with something of a surprise that he brought Vanessa's head around.

"Tell me, my beauty, do you often go about the countryside in breeches at the dead of night?"

She was shocked and taken aback. She stared at his face, found his eyes and in their gray dark depths saw a certain danger. What then? Had he seen her? She answered cautiously, "Sometimes."

He threw back his head and let go a laugh. When next he moved forward it was to take her chin in his hand. "Very good, Vanessa. Never lie when there is a good chance you might be caught at it. You are wondering how I came by my information?" He moved closer to her still. Egad, he thought, her nearness is making it hard to concentrate on anything but her lips. "You are all too beautiful to miss, riding across the moors on that gray of yours. Where had you been?"

"Meeting my lover clandestinely, of course," she returned demurely. "Where else should I have been at such an hour?"

Now he was taken aback. He studied her and decided she was teasing him. "Then I am ill with jealously and mean to do the devil in!"

"An excellent notion, for I was growing rather tired of the brute. These farmer's sons are divinely built but lack conversation, you see."

He let go a laugh. "You almost make me believe that was what you were doing."

"It is what you thought—why then don't you believe it when you hear it?" she returned, lifting her brow, allowing her pursed lips a curve.

She was enchanting. "Somehow I can't conceive a picture of you in some farmer's arms."

"But I dressed the part. I had on my breeches!" objected Vanessa.

"Oh love, if I thought for a moment any man had won you ... I would do him in," said Duncan, now very serious.

200

"Well, then you are spared the effort, for no man calls me his," said Vanessa archly.

"What then? Were you just out for a ride? Does Lady Penrod allow it?"

"No, she does not, but yes, I was just out for a ride. I am a free soul, Duncan. If I were a man, no one would give a brace of snaps whether I chose to take a midnight ride. It is infuriating to think that because I am a woman I must slink around. I enjoy riding... and what's more, I enjoy riding in breeches. I am at best a most reprehensible creature. A sore trial to my parents." She let go an admirable sigh.

"If you were mine, I should let you ride about in breeches and adore the essence of your mind that urges you to such activity. I should allow you anything you desire."

"Anything?" she teased.

"Anything!" he returned earnestly.

"No, I think not. You see, I am destined to be a veritable shrew, intolerable to any man's peace of mind," she declared lightly.

"Then be one to me. Cut up my peace if you will, Vanessa, but allow me to call you mine," pleaded Duncan, taking up her shoulders and allowing her to see the sweet passion on his face.

She attempted to return to the safety of a light flirtation. "And sir... are you making me an improper proposal?" Her lips were curved deliciously.

He wanted to kiss her. She moved him to feel... whether it was love he didn't know, didn't care. He only knew she tantalized him with her lips, her movements, her eyes. "Yes, for I mean to love you most improperly for a man and wife in our age!"

She pulled out of his touch, for she could see he meant to show her just what he had in mind. She got to her feet. "I think, Duncan, this has gone far enough.

You know not what you are saying, and are carried away by this moment."

He stood up with her and once again had her elegant shoulders.

"Vanessa . . . I am carried away, but not by any moment. By you, Vanessa . . . only by you."

"Stop it! Duncan, we have only just met."

"And yet I knew in that meeting that I had to have you. You are the only woman for me, Vanessa . . ."

"Then I am sorry to hear it, for . . . I am not ready to call any man husband."

"You will be. I will make you want me . . . love me."

"Will you? Well then . . . we shall see. But for the time being I must ask you not to go on in this fashion . . . you are making me uncomfortable, and that, my dear sir, cannot do your cause any good!"

He searched her face a moment, dropped his hands to his sides. Yes, he could see he had been precipitate in his proposal. "Come then, we have a great deal more ground to cover, you and I."

"Well, not all in one day, sir, for then I shall have no excuse to return tomorrow," she said lightly. She wanted to cut this short. She wanted to return to Penrod, tack up her horse and ride to a certain cave and speak with a certain man. In fact, she found it very difficult to think of anything else. For a fleeting moment she wondered what she would have answered had Montlaine asked her to wed. Preposterous! Montlaine was a . . . a rogue!

Chapter Seventeen

The gold sitting room at Penrod tower was decorated with cheerfulness in mind. The trimmings, the china bric-a-brac, the paintings, were all set and chosen to give an overall brightness to the room. Its occupants at this particular moment were not affected by their surroundings, and the sense of doom permeated the air.

Edward Parks, having greeted young Mary, whom he had a special fondness for, went then to examine the weapon. This brought on a black air of consternation. He shot questions at Richard, who eventually took affront. He more gently shot questions at Bess Widdons, who took to the settee and showed signs of going off once again into a faint. Only Mary seemed to maintain an air of calm, but as she took to holding Parks's arm and keeping in step with him as he paced to and fro, Richard called out irritably, "I think your attitude is very lax, girl, and do let go of Mr. Parks and come here and sit down!"

"Well, my attitude may not be what you like, Richard, but at least I am not allowing my chin to fall to the ground with worry. And as to letting go of Edward's arm, I won't. He is a very dear friend and I have missed him terribly." She looked up at Edward Parks and said quietly, "We both loved Bret . . . very much."

Parks smiled at her and patted her hand comfortingly. Something had to be done. If Duncan had been so blatant as to take a chance out in the open, this Widdons girl must know something.

"Mary, I am off now . . . for there is something I have to attend to. But I don't want Miss Widdons to leave here . . . I should like to question her later, when she is feeling more the thing."

"As to that, Parks, we had no intention of allowing her to leave!" returned Richard, taking umbrage again. He had no liking for the way the fellow had just come in and taken over. After all, his sister had left him in charge, and that was the way he wanted it!

"Good," said Parks, turning again to Mary, "Stay close to the house, child."

"Oh, don't worry. After all, Richard is protecting me," said Mary shyly.

Richard preened and felt inclined to be gracious enough to show Parks to the front door, where they met Lady Penrod coming in. She put up a brow in surprise. "Why, Edward . . . you here?"

He smiled. "Yes, but I am just leaving, my lady. A great deal has occurred that you will want to know about. Richard here will, I am sure, put you in way of the facts, as I must be rushing off."

"Oh? Oh . . . very well . . ."

Richard linked his arm through Lady Penrod's and began portentously, "You see, ma'am . . ."

Parks had but one aim. It was dangerous, for it was the middle of the day and he might be seen. He would have to be careful. He rode his horse toward the moors and over their terrain, making for the viscount of Montlaine.

Some ten minutes later had him leading his horse down the narrow stretch of beach, where he saw the viscount walking his stallion. He shook his head and called out, "Bret, for the love of . . . what the deuce are you doing in broad daylight?"

"Poor Midnight came up stiff this morning when I was lunging him. Odd thing, seems sound now, though." He grinned. "But what brings you this fine day, Edward?"

Parks ignored this and put his horse's reins into his friend's capable hands. "Which leg?"

"Right fore."

Parks ran his hand over the horse's legs and stopped just above the hoof for a moment. "I can't feel any heat, Bret."

"No, nor could I. I couldn't find any heat or pain in his shoulder . . . but no matter, he is quite sound this morning. I daresay it was just a spasm."

"Well then, come on, my man, put the horse away. We have got to talk," returned Parks, dismissing the subject of horses and getting on with the point at hand.

"Eh? Sounds like trouble."

"And so it is. You won't like it," said Parks, following the viscount into the cave.

The stallion took strong exception to Parks's gelding and would have kicked back at the horse had not the viscount sensed what was coming and kept the two apart while he stalled his animal.

"Secure your horse up by the cave mouth, Edward. You'll find a handy ring set in the stone."

This done, Parks returned and dived headlong into the matter that had brought him. "Bret . . . one of the

205

Echworths, Duncan, I think, has taken a go at Mary!"

"What? Devil you say!" thundered the viscount of Montlaine.

"At least, we think it may have been Mary he was aiming at." He scratched at his ear and his face was drawn in consternation. "I shall give it to you as best I can. Lady Vanessa came in upon us at Montlaine..."

"Vanessa...at Montlaine? Came in on who?"

"I was with Duncan, attempting to get him to commit himself to me...when Vanessa arrived alone. She gave out this story about someone taking aim at Mary...I am afraid I blundered and took away her bait."

"What do you mean?"

"I have a strong notion she was trying to trap Duncan into mentioning the knife..."

"The knife? Fiend seize your prattle! Explain all this!" shouted the viscount, goaded beyond endurance.

"Listen, then. Someone, using a knife, took aim and missed Mary in the woods bordering Penrod."

"What in hell was she doing in the woods?"

"Let me start at the beginning. I was attempting to explain that Vanessa came up to Montlaine I believe with the express purpose of trying to trap Duncan into an admission. I am afraid I foiled it."

"What makes you say she came to Montlaine for that purpose?" The viscount was frowning darkly.

"For one thing, she is not as dumb, nor as frightened as she pretended to be. For another, she gave over that she thought the attempt was made at Mary..."

"But that is what you have just said yourself?"

"Yes, well, you have not allowed me to tell the whole. If you won't stop interrupting, Bret, we shall never get to the meat of it."

"Go on before I wring your neck, Edward," said Bret sweetly.

"She gave over at Montlaine that she thought the knife was meant for Mary, yet her brother and Mary say that she believes it was meant for Bess Widdons!"

"I shall go mad!" declared the viscount. "What in blazes has Bess Widdons to do with any of this?"

"That is another thing. She told Duncan that Bess came to see Mary...when Mary tells me it was Vanessa who arranged the thing. So you see, I blundered badly when I brought up the gun..."

"What gun?"

"Never mind, there wasn't any. Here, calm yourself, Bret, and allow me to explain."

Slowly, carefully and in intelligent prose Edward recounted the tale as he knew it. He then removed his hat, wiped his brow with his handkerchief and said gently that things were moving too fast and that Duncan was the very personification of wickedness to have such greed working at him.

The viscount paced furiously, and then when he turned to stare at his friend, Parks could see that the black eyes were lit with dangerous glints of fire.

"Damn his soul! He'll not touch Mary...no, nor Vanessa either, for he has plans in that direction. The time has come for me to show myself, Edward." He picked up his cloak, spied Vanessa's lying near his straw bed and picked it up too. "Besides, I have an errand to run!"

"But Bret...you can't mean it? What good will it do for you to come out in the open? No, not now when we are so close," objected Parks fretfully.

"Because as long as he thinks me dead, Mary will be a target. She is next in line, you see. He can't get his hands on the total inheritance until Mary is disposed of. First he will have to see me tried and hung."

"And so he will. Don't be a fool. Your coming out now will only serve to stall for time."

"I think not, Edward. There is something I can do with Bess Widdons that none of you can."

"Which is what?"

"Frighten her into telling us what she knows... or wait a minute! Why the deuce didn't I think of it earlier?" He turned with some excitement. "*It will work, Parks*... it has got to work!"

"What? What has to work?"

"I'll tell you on the way to Penrod. Now, old friend, are you with me?"

"I don't know how it is, but as always, Bret... I am with you!"

Chapter Eighteen

"There now, Miss Widdons, perhaps you are sufficiently recovered to partake of tea with Mary and me," said Lady Penrod gently. She had only just come in on the scene and was still rather confused over the details.

"Thank you . . . you have been very kind," returned Bess, still avoiding Mary's eye.

"Kinder than you have been to us!" put in Mary as she discontinued her stomping around the room to take up a position beside Lady Penrod and stare Bess down.

"How can you sit there and drink tea in this house? How can you be so . . . guiltless?" demanded Mary as Bess attempted to ignore her.

"Someone tried to kill me today . . . doesn't that make you understand?" cried Bess, at last answering back.

"So, the chit has a tongue!" said Mary. "Excellent. Perhaps there is a mind behind the tongue. Think, Bess, if he tried to kill you today . . . won't he keep on trying? He doesn't realize how stubborn you are. He doesn't realize that you aren't telling us what you know!"

"Oh...oh...dear..." This from Bess, who buried her face in her hands.

"Good lord, she has gone off again!" cried Mary on a note of frustration. "Every time I think I am getting through to her, she starts moaning!"

"Hush, Mary. That is enough. Allow the child to drink her tea in peace. Perhaps it will give her a different perspective on the issue at hand," said Lady Penrod assuagingly. She put her own hand to her forehead and closed her eyes. This was all getting to be quite an ordeal. When would it end?

At this point the sitting-room doors were flung open, and filling its wide portal stood a tall and exceptionally broad-shouldered young man. His long black waves fell over his forehead and down around his ears in wild profusion. His white shirt was open nearly to the waist beneath his dark cloak. His dark breeches displayed athletic thighs. His high Hessian boots were covered in dust. All this made a striking picture and cowed the room into awed silence. Added to his surprising arrival, the belief the present occupants of the second-floor sitting room had that he was dead made him all the more imposing.

Mary let go a shriek after her initial shock and ran crying, sobbing and laughing into his arms. "I knew it! I knew you couldn't be dead. *Not you.* I kept sneaking out to Bodmin Heights in hopes, I just couldn't believe...oh, Bret...Bret!"

Lady Penrod put her vinaigrette to her nose and took a decided whiff. The room seemed slightly off balance. Was she dreaming? Was this really the viscount or some terrible trick?

With his arm still about his sister's waist, he moved toward her ladyship and bent low over her hand.

"Guss...I am so sorry if I have overwhelmed you."

She touched him affectionately. "A more pleasant shock I couldn't want...and isn't it just like you to do such a thing to us?"

Parks heard a sound behind him and turned to find Richard and his cousin coming up the stairs. However, Bess let go a long wail, which once again turned the viscount's attention. Richard and Randall heard the cry as well and rushed to enter the sitting room.

"What? Is that girl off again? Come on, Rand...she is no doubt driving Mary to murder, and I tell you frankly I won't have it!"

They entered the room, passed up Parks with a nod and stopped short to stare at the viscount leaning over Bess's hand. Randall poked his cousin in the ribs,

"Thunder and turf, old boy...ain't that the dead fellow in the portrait?"

"Well, and he ain't dead," returned Ricky reasonably. "I mean, Randy, really...anybody can see that." He didn't bother explaining that he had known this fact since last night.

"No...but...shouldn't he be?" returned his cousin in confusion.

"Be quiet!" ordered Parks. "I can't hear what he is saying to Bess."

"There now, Bess...hush, girl...I am not blaming you. No one is, but if you feel it is in your power to help us and you don't...won't you blame yourself?"

"I...I don't know if I can help. You see...I only know what Melony told me," sobbed Bess.

"Which is hearsay and is inadmissible in court," said Parks. "You see, Bess has no way of proving that Melony actually told her...though we might make some use of it..."

"Who was the father of Melony's child? Who, Bess?" pursued the viscount. He would know if only for his own satisfaction.

"Duncan..." It was a whisper.

The viscount frowned. "But that, my dear, is quite impossible. We have it on good authority that Duncan was in London."

"No...no, he wasn't. Melony said that they had switched places...Duncan and Orson...that Orson didn't even know about the cult meetings."

Once again the sitting-room door opened, and this time it was Vanessa with Duncan close behind that silenced the occupants.

Vanessa saw the viscount at once and sucked in breath. What had happened? Why was he here? Her first thought was to protect him from Duncan, and she moved to block Duncan's line of vision.

She took hold of Duncan's arm and said as merrily as she could muster, "Oh, Duncan...I had almost forgotten. There is something I have been wanting to show you..." She attempted to pull him around, but it was too late, for he had already taken in the vision of the viscount on one knee and leaning very near to Bess Widdons!

Duncan was momentarily bereft of speech. The viscount? Alive? What then? Why had he been pretending to be dead? Why had he decided to come out in the open? What had Bess Widdons told him? What to do? What to do? No proof! Bess Widdons had no proof!

He managed an admirable sneer, considering his shock, and said quite casually, "Well, well, so my cousin returns from the dead? Certainly a sorcerer's trick."

Richard went to Mary and stuck her behind his elbow in a corner of the room. As far as he was concerned, Mary was the target here. Randall frowned and pressed closer to Edward Parks and whispered, "There's bound to be a famous set-to now!"

"Hmmm. I should think so," agreed Parks.

Lady Penrod attempted to assuage the flaring tempers. "Ah, Duncan, I am certain you are in need of refreshments. Shall I ring for some?"

She was ignored, for Duncan and the viscount had a score to settle. The viscount noted that Vanessa's hand still clutched at Duncan's arm and he frowned darkly. "Vanessa, come here if you will."

She wanted to placate him, and though usually a command such as this would have served only to make her do just the opposite, she thought it wise to comply for the time being. However, Duncan would not have it. He reached out, found her hand and drew her near. His eyes were reproachful when he looked down at her.

"It appears that you are acquainted with my cousin? Is he then your farmer's son for whom you wore the breeches?"

She frowned. "You overstep, sir!"

The viscount took a stride forward. His black eyes were stormy, and it appeared to the company at large that he might lose himself and set his fives into Duncan's face. However, his better sense won out. "And did you force poor Melony to your side thus?" He gestured at the manner in which Duncan held Vanessa near. "But then you didn't count on Bess Widdons, did you? No, you hadn't realized that when the two were not putting their heads together about you, they were *corresponding!* That is right. You see, Duncan, although Bess did not want her parents to discover her part in your cult meetings on the moors, she has decided that she can keep silent no longer!"

"You are bluffing! She has only hearsay!" shouted Duncan.

213

"No...she has a letter, written by Melony, that names you father of her child," said the viscount slowly.

Vanessa sucked in breath, but there was little time for ought else. Duncan acted quickly, devastatingly. Before she knew what he was about he had brought a slender crystal vase crashing down upon the table. The resonance of breaking glass startled enough people in the room to still them while he brought up the jagged piece of the vase to Vanessa's throat and forced her to back up with him. "No one move!" he commanded. "I should hate to spill this beauty's blood, but mark me...I will, if only for spite."

They reached the sitting-room door. He hooked Vanessa around the throat with his elbow, and his hand pointed the serrated vase at her face so that she was very still. His free hand felt behind him for the key. Large, brass and resting in the keyhole, this was discovered easily enough. He took it out and then opened the door, pulling Vanessa roughly out with him. Once there he planted her against the wall, and though the viscount rushed the door from the other side it was too late. The latch was in place, the key inserted and turned.

Again he had Vanessa, this time one hand around her waist and the other still pointing the jagged glass at her throat. One of its sharper points did in fact scratch her, and she felt her warm blood ooze out. Even for Vanessa it was a frightening experience and seemed to take the fight out of her.

His arm relaxed a moment, and she attempted to kick at him. He had not the patience to put up with such, and with the blunt bottom of the crystal he sent a blow across the back of her neck that did the job he required.

Vanessa saw shooting stars in a black velvet sky,

red and brilliant white explosions, as she slumped into unconsciousness. He scooped her up and hurried to the stables with the tale that she was ill. Quickly, he laid her into the unicorn curricle, which had not yet been unhitched. His own horse he left behind as he cracked the whip and sent the curricle forward at a spanking pace.

Within the sitting room a commotion of some magnitude had ensued. The viscount was attempting to break the door down. Richard and Randall were shouting for Toby at the top of their lungs. Edward Parks was attempting to open one of the windows, which he managed to do before Toby arrived on the scene.

The viscount rushed to the window, ignored the fact that they were at some distance above the ground and proceeded to lower himself by his arms, thereby reducing the distance, before he dropped to his feet. He landed heavily, for he was a large man and took the brunt of it in his ankles, but he paid this no heed as he rushed around the house in time to see Duncan making his hasty escape. However, it was not this that drained the color from the viscount's face. He could see Vanessa in an unconscious heap on the seat beside Duncan.

A moment later saw him astride Midnight and in concerted pursuit. His nerves were taut with determination, and his will was centered in but one effort, to get his Vanessa safely within his protection and do away with Duncan once and for all!

Duncan took his corners dangerously. Speed! The curricle was designed for it, but then too it was designed to be used in such a manner only by a notable whip. The late Lord Penrod had been such a man, but

215

Duncan was not. He handled the reins badly, and the blood gelding began frothing at the mouth. The horse threw up his head in anger at the misuse of the ribbons, but Duncan came down hard with the whip, sending the horse onward.

Vanessa began floating in semiconsciousness. Her head ached terribly, her neck felt stiff, her body seemed to be rocking dreadfully. She attempted to rise, felt as though she might swoon and remained still a moment longer. Then she heard Duncan shouting at the horse, calling for more speed, and it all came back to her in a sweeping blast of horror. She forced herself to sit up and immediately wished she had not. She held the sides of the curricle bench for support as they rounded a corner, and she objected, "You will overturn us, Duncan... you must slow down for the bends..."

"Jade!" he returned. "All this time ... you have been doing me up sweet and slinking out to see *him* ... work with *him!*"

"Doing you up sweet? Good gracious..." she exclaimed, her hand still pressing the back of her neck. "You weren't even here until yesterday." There were exploding fireworks in her head, and the road ahead seemed blurred and indistinct. She attempted to focus.

"Was I not? Oh yes, the fine distinction. You see ... I played the part of poor Orson until last night."

"Did you? But why? I don't understand."

He sneered. "No, you wouldn't. My twin is a bit squeamish about taking action. He would rather leave things to the fates. I knew he would never organize a cult ... put it at Bret's door ... so I sent him off to London to take my place. We have often switched places. He did it without question ... he never questions me. I took over here, and in secret got up twelve girls and we played at devilry on the moors. It was a lark to

216

them ... it was a purpose to an end for me. When Melony started her attack, I turned it to purpose as well. I gave the girl a poison and put in her hand Bret's pendant, which I had taken days before to leave at one of our cult meetings in the circle." He shook his head angrily. "I didn't count on the Widdons girl ... never thought ..."

"Give it all up, Duncan. Let me go. It will delay them long enough to give you a respite to think ... to get away ..."

"Let you go?" he returned incredulously. "I see you haven't fathomed my way of thinking yet, pretty woman. No, you are my escape! Your father is a Grey. There is nothing he wouldn't do to protect your name and that of your husband. I intend to make you my wife. Your father will manage to hush up the affair while we take our honeymoon in Italy ... I shan't have to go to trial ..."

"You have quite lost your mind!" said Vanessa in disgust. "There is no way you can force me to marry you."

"Is there not? We shall see, my love. Indeed, we shall see."

She stared at him and became truly frightened. He was dangerous, his earlier behavior told just how very dangerous, and now apparently he had worked out some wicked scheme involving herself. She had to escape ... but how? She could break her neck if she were to jump from the unicorn now!

The viscount found himself at the fork in the road. One led toward the village, the other inland. He studied the ground until he found the tracks he was looking for. So, Duncan was traveling inland. To what purpose? Bret knew the land far better than his cousin. He smiled as he reached a portion of fence flanking the road and sent his horse flying over its height. Through the field, over the meadow cutting the road and back once again over the fence to wait for Duncan's arrival.

He heard them coming before he saw them and got into position. Duncan saw the devil himself blocking his path and blinked in some confusion. It was impossible. How could he be here before him? It just wasn't possible. He was transfixed with indecision, and Vanessa took the opportunity to repay him for his earlier brutality. He had discarded the broken vase in the back of the curricle. She managed in the space of the moment to take it up and bring it down hard over his head. It dazed him but did not put him out; however, it was enough to stall for time. His hold on the ribbons slackened. Vanessa took them up and pulled them in. At the same time she reached over and yanked on the brake.

Nothing more was needed. The viscount was on Duncan in that moment. He lifted him with one hand and landed him a settler that sent him flying off the carriage. The viscount followed him, picked him up by his buckskin lapels and planted his closed fives in Duncan's belly before bringing his fist up quickly across his bonebox.

Vanessa saw the blood spurt out of Duncan's mouth, saw the man's eyes haze over and close. She ran to the viscount and stayed his arm with her imploring hands.

"Enough! Oh, my love, it is enough . . . he is unconscious!"

The viscount was dimly aware that the man he dropped was in no fit condition for more. However, what stopped him was Vanessa's words. He turned to her. "You called me your love . . ." With which he took her into his arms. She was here, she was bright and feisty, and what was more . . . she was his! His lips touched her forehead and treaded wildly across her face, making haste to reach her lips.

Vanessa clung to him, returned his kisses, and at last when he allowed her breath, she said, "Oh, Bret . . . but, we are forgetting Duncan. What will you do with him?"

"Edward has by now no doubt sent for the magistrate. We will return with Duncan to Penrod, where I shall put my cousin into custody." He touched the bruise already turning colors on her neck, traced the dried blood near her throat, and his lips drew together tightly. He looked as though he might start pummeling Duncan once again, but Vanessa turned his cheek toward her and kissed his fingers.

"'Tis the veriest scratch . . . oh, Bret, the nightmare is over!"

"And the dream, my sweetheart, begins! Vanessa, I love you, want you for my bride . . ."

"Thank goodness," said the lady brightly. "Now, if you please, sir, we must do something with Duncan, for I believe he is about to stir, and there is, I think, a carriage coming down the road."

The viscount of Montlaine paid not the slightest heed to either of these incidentals as he took his love very tightly into his arms and proceeded to display the depth of his feelings.

What then happened to the Echworths? Montlaine, at the insistence of his bride-to-be, provided Sheila and her mother with a small but comfortable establishment in the wilds of northern Scotland. Orson too was allowed after a minor term of imprisonment to join them there. Duncan, however, was found guilty of the murder of Melony Fry and for his crime was publicly hanged.

Edward Parks, satisified that justice had been done, returned to his prospering law practice and looked about himself for a wife. Richard and Randall accompanied Vanessa and Montlaine to Brighton, where the young couple were wed. Needless to say, the wedding served to envelop Vanessa's parents with unlimited joy and an even greater hope of her rehabilitation. Lady Penrod returned happily to the social scene, and thus we are left only with Mary of Montlaine . . . ah, but then that is another tale altogether!

About the author:

Claudette Williams was born in Baghdad, and immigrated to the United States when she was two years old. She researches extensively for her novels, traveling to a Barbados plantation and to historical sites in Virginia for her book PASSION'S PRIDE. She now lives on Long Island with her husband, an electrical contractor, and her seven-year-old daughter.